'Is it a deal?'

'I—guess it has to b

'Graciously spoken, as always,' he murmured. 'What did you do with your wedding ring?'

'It's in my pocket.'

Gabriel held out a hand. 'Give it to me.'

He slid the ring onto her finger.

'I'm sure you've no wish to repeat our vows… However, I feel I should seal this solemn moment somehow… So, I'll kiss the bride.'

She wanted to say no—to pull away. But the arms that closed round her were too strong, too determined. And his mouth was too warm, too compelling, stifling the rejection before it could be uttered.

He kissed her slowly and sensuously, as if he had all the time in the world. Joanna felt her whole body shiver in a response she was unable to control.

When he lifted his head, he was smiling.

He said lightly, 'If I didn't know better, Jo, I'd swear you almost enjoyed that.'

Sara Craven was born in South Devon, and grew up surrounded by books, in a house by the sea. After leaving grammar school she worked as a local journalist, covering everything from flower shows to murders. She started writing for Mills & Boon® in 1975. Apart from writing, her passions include films, music, cooking and eating in good restaurants. She now lives in Somerset.

Sara Craven has appeared as a contestant on the Channel Four game show *Fifteen to One* and in 1997 she became the winner of the 25th and final *Mastermind of Great Britain* title.

Recent titles by the same author:

ONE RECKLESS NIGHT
A NANNY FOR CHRISTMAS

MARRIAGE AT A DISTANCE

BY
SARA CRAVEN

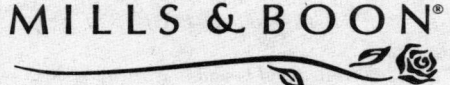

MILLS & BOON®

*First published in Great Britain 1998
Harlequin Mills & Boon Limited,
Eton House, 18-24 Paradise Road, Richmond, Surrey TW9 1SR*

© Sara Craven 1998

ISBN 0 263 81058 5

*Set in Times Roman 11 on 11½ pt.
01-9808-46945 C1*

*Printed and bound in Norway
by AiT Trondheim AS, Trondheim*

CHAPTER ONE

THE air in the study was stale and cold. It was gloomy, too, with the curtains at the long windows half drawn against a February dusk.

But the girl who sat curled up in the big leather chair beside the fireplace had not switched on any of the lamps, or lit the neatly laid fire waiting in the grate.

Her only response to the chill in the room had been to spread an old velvet smoking jacket over her legs like a rug. And every so often she looked down at it, touching the worn pile gently, breathing the faint aroma of cigars that rose from it.

Impossible to think that Lionel would never wear it again. That he would never come in through that door, large, loud and unrelentingly kind, rubbing his hands together and exclaiming about the weather, his face red from tramping over the hills with the dogs, or riding out on his latest hunter.

When the new chestnut had come back yesterday without him, Sadie, his girl groom, had said dourly that she'd warned him the horse was too fresh. But the worst they'd expected was that Lionel had been thrown, perhaps suffered a broken collarbone.

Instead, as Dr Fraser had told them, the massive heart attack that he'd suffered had probably knocked him from the saddle. It was also, he'd added gently, the way Lionel would have wanted to go.

Joanna could accept that. Lionel had always been restless, she thought. Always active. Since his retirement as chairman of Verne Investments five years ago, he'd been forever looking for ways to fill his days. He would never have wanted to be chronically ill, perhaps bedridden, the rush and bustle he'd thrived on denied him.

But that did not make it any less of a shock for those left behind, she thought, the muscles in her throat tightening.

And the question endlessly revolving in her tired mind was, What's going to happen to me now?

Because Lionel's death had changed everything. Taken all the old certainties away with him.

Until yesterday she'd been Joanna Verne, his daughter-in-law. The girl who ran the house for him and dealt with all the boring domestic issues he hated to be plagued with.

Twenty-four hours later she was little better than a displaced person. The estranged wife of Lionel's son and heir, Gabriel Verne, who had spent the last two years of their inimical separation storming round the globe, building on the success of Verne Investments, turning his father and himself from the merely rich to the mega-rich.

Gabriel, who would now be coming back to claim Westroe Manor, and also to rid himself finally of the wife he'd never wanted. And her stepmother, she acknowledged wryly.

In the distance she heard the doorbell jangle, and she pushed the encumbering folds of the jacket away and got to her feet.

She'd asked Henry Fortescue, Lionel's solicitor, to call, and she didn't want him to find her lurking here in the dark like this. She owed it to herself—and to Lionel—to put a brave face on things.

She moved swiftly, rattling the curtains along their

poles to exclude the last remnants of grey daylight, switching on the central pendant, and kneeling to put a match to the kindling. By the time Mr Fortescue was shown into the room by Mrs Ashby, the flames were licking at the coal and the study looked altogether more cheerful.

Henry Fortescue's face was strained and sad. He and Lionel had been close since boyhood, she remembered sympathetically as she rose from the hearthrug, dusting her hands on her denim jeans.

He came across to her and took her hand. 'Joanna, my dear. I'm so sorry—so very sorry. I can still hardly believe it.'

'Nor I.' She patted his sleeve. 'I'm going to have a whisky. Will you join me?'

The surprise on his face brought a reluctant smile to her lips. She said with gentle irony, 'I am old enough. And I think we could both do with one.'

'And I'm sure you're right.' He smiled back at her with an effort. 'But only a very small one, please. I'm driving.'

'Highland water with it?' Joanna busied herself with the decanter and glasses on a corner table.

'Oh, yes. I wouldn't insult Lionel's memory by diluting his best malt with soda.'

He raised the glass she handed him with slight awkwardness. 'What shall we drink to?'

'I think—absent friends, don't you?' They shared the toast, then sat opposite each other on either side of the fireplace.

After a pause, he said, 'And how is Mrs Elcott?'

Joanna bit her lip. 'In her room. She's—devastated.'

'I'm sure she is,' Henry Fortescue said with a certain dryness. 'It must be intensely frustrating for her to know that her hopes will never now be fulfilled.'

Joanna raised her eyebrows. 'That, dearest Mr Fortescue, was almost indiscreet,' she observed with mock reproof.

'I intended it to be,' he returned robustly. 'I knew exactly what she was after and I didn't like it, either as Lionel's friend or his lawyer.'

Joanna sighed. 'Lionel, as we both know, was too kind for his own good. Look how he's always treated me.'

He frowned. 'I hope you're not equating your situation with your stepmother's. It was perfectly natural for Lionel to offer you a home after your father died. Your mother was his favourite cousin, after all. But Cynthia had no claim on his generosity at all. Why, she and Jeremy had only been married a matter of months when the accident happened. She was a total stranger to him.'

He shook his head sternly. 'She was a young, healthy woman. Still is, for that matter. There was nothing to prevent her finding another secretarial job—making a life for herself. But instead she moved herself in here—on your coat-tails, as it were.' He snorted. 'She should have been the one running the house all this time. I know that was Lionel's intention.'

'Oh, I never minded.' Joanna tasted her drink, savouring the smoky warmth caressing her throat. 'Besides, housekeeping has never been Cynthia's forte.'

'And what is?' His tone was sceptical.

Joanna wrinkled her nose. 'Being decorative, I suppose.'

Which I never was, she thought with a pang of pain, remembering her shrinking teen self waiting to be introduced to her father's new wife, only to be devastated by a sweeping, dismissive look and a laughing, 'Goodness, what a Plain Jane'.

'Anyway, none of it will be for much longer,' Joanna went on hurriedly. 'I hope she hasn't lost her secretarial skills, at least, because I can't see Gabriel allowing her to become his pensioner.' She paused. 'Or myself, of course.'

Mr Fortescue shifted uncomfortably. 'Joanna—Mrs Verne—you will naturally have certain rights...'

'Alimony—things like that.' She forced a smile. 'I don't want them. And please don't call me Mrs Verne. I'm reverting to my maiden name as from now.'

'Is that really necessary?' He sounded troubled.

'Yes,' Joanna said calmly. 'Oh, yes.' She looked down at the amber liquid in her glass. 'The main reason I asked you here this evening was to beg a favour. I want you to forward a letter from me to Gabriel. Obviously you'll be in touch with him, and I—I'm not.'

She bit her lip. 'While Lionel was here it was impossible to discuss divorce. You know how he felt about it. But everything's different now.'

He looked at her gravely. 'I know he always hoped that you and Gabriel would be reconciled. He blamed himself very much for the breakdown in your relationship. Felt he'd pushed you both into marriage before you were ready.'

Joanna sat up rather straighter. She said crisply, 'Even if Gabriel and I had gone through a ten-year engagement with a cooling-off period, it would still have been a disaster. We were completely unsuited.'

She got to her feet and went over to the desk, picking up a sealed envelope. 'I'm offering him a quick, clean-break divorce with no blame attached on either side.' Her smile was small and wintry. 'Considering his mileage in the gossip columns over the past two years, I call that generous.'

He said forcefully, 'As a lawyer, I call it foolhardy.'

'Ah, but you're Gabriel's lawyer now, not mine, remember.' She handed him the envelope. 'If you would forward it for me, I'd be glad. There's no reason to delay any longer.'

He looked down at the letter, frowning a little. 'Or you could always give it to him yourself.' He paused, his gaze direct, almost compassionate. 'You do realise that he's coming back for the funeral.'

Joanna could feel the colour drain from her face. 'I didn't think he would. Not after that terrible quarrel before he left,' she said at last. 'Stupid of me.'

'However bitter the feelings at the time, my dear, Gabriel would hardly absent himself at a time like this. Lionel was loved and respected by the local people, and any sign of disrespect, particularly from his heir, would cause a lot of resentment.'

'Yes,' she said. 'Yes, of course.' A small harsh laugh choked its way out of her. 'I—I had no idea he cared so much for the conventions.'

'He's now the owner of Westroe Manor. He knows his obligations.'

She said icily, 'That is not a word I associate with my former husband.'

She saw a shadow of disapproval on his face, and resumed her seat. 'I'm sorry. I'm a bit thrown, that's all. I just thought—I assumed that I'd be allowed a little time—some leeway—to make my own plans before his return.'

'What are your plans?' His voice was gentle.

'I don't know yet.' Joanna shook her head. 'I keep

trying to think—to decide something. But my mind just goes round in circles.'

'It's early days.'

'Ah, no,' she said. 'You've just proved to me that it's later than I think. I shall really have to concentrate.' She paused. 'Do you know—have you heard when Gabriel is due?'

'I believe,' he said carefully, 'that he will be here the day after tomorrow.' He hesitated. 'He has asked for the reading of the will to be delayed until after the funeral.'

'How very traditional.' Joanna gripped her hands together in her lap, aware that they were shaking. 'He really does mean to play Lord of the Manor.'

'I don't think there was ever any doubt of that.' Henry Fortescue finished his whisky and put the tumbler aside. 'Do you still wish me to deliver your letter?'

'Under the circumstances, it's probably easier for me to do it myself,' she acknowledged wearily. 'I'm sorry for wasting your time.'

'You never do that, Joanna. And I intended to call on you, anyway.' He shook hands with her, gravely studying her pale face and shadowed eyes. 'A word of advice,' he added gently. 'I wouldn't be too hasty about dropping your husband's name, at least until the funeral is over. Remember what I said about local opinion. The next few days are bound to be hard enough, without creating extra difficulties—resentments—for yourself.'

'Yes,' she said, almost inaudibly. 'I'm sure you're right. Thank you.'

'I'll see myself out.' He patted her hand and went. Presently she heard him talking to Mrs Ashby, and then the sound of the front door closing.

She leaned back in the big chair. It wasn't just her hands any more. Her whole body was trembling violently—uncontrollably.

The shock of Lionel's sudden death had stunned her into overlooking its most direct consequence, she realised numbly.

Gabriel hadn't been near Westroe Manor for two years, making the breach between them absolute, and she'd presumed he would take his time over his return, that he would be too busy being the Superman of the financial world all day and the playboy of the western world all night to concern himself with his old home. Especially a home that contained his unwanted and discarded wife.

Did he even know that she was still living there? she wondered. Or that she'd been managing the house and staff for his father?

But of course he did, she corrected herself derisively. Gabriel made it his business to know everything.

A sudden image of his thin, dark face, with those insolent, heavy-lidded eyes, tawny as a leopard's, and that narrow-lipped, mocking mouth flared into her mind, and was instantly dismissed.

She did not want to remember Gabriel's mouth, or his hands, or the lean, vibrant body which had so fleetingly made her his possession.

The events of the few brief nights she'd spent with him were stamped on her consciousness for ever, however many times she'd tried to erase them. And so were the contemptuous words with which he'd finally ended them.

'I think I'll do us both a favour, and find some other form of entertainment.' His icy drawl had cut across her quivering senses like the lash of a whip.

And he'd been as good as his word, she thought bitterly. He'd made no secret of his infidelities, staying away for longer and longer periods that even Lionel could not pretend had any connection with work any more.

And then, one day, Gabriel had returned. But only to collect the rest of his things. He was leaving, he said, permanently this time.

Inevitably there'd been a showdown—one blazing, terrifying row. Father and son had faced each other like enemies. Harsh, unforgivable things had been said on both sides, while she'd crouched between them, her hands over her ears, begging them to stop.

'You'll stay here, damn you,' Lionel had roared. 'And do your duty by your wife—if she's prepared to forgive you. Or you'll never enter this house again.'

She'd looked up at Gabriel, her lips mutely forming the word 'Please', not knowing even then if she was begging him to go or to stay. The tawny eyes had flicked over her, bathing her in flame.

Then: 'I'm sorry,' Gabriel said derisively. 'But there are some sacrifices no man should be called on to make.'

And he'd gone.

She'd wanted to go too, distressed at the trouble the failure of their marriage had caused and tormented by her memories, but Lionel had forbidden it.

'You're my daughter-in-law, and the mistress of this house,' he'd stated, his tone brooking no opposition. 'Your home remains here.'

But perhaps she should have stood up to him. Insisted on leaving. Her final school examination results had been respectable enough to win her a training course at a polytechnic, if not a place at university. By now she could have embarked on a career. Had a life of her own. But she'd stayed, feeling that she owed Lionel something more than loyalty, because he'd placed himself at odds with his only son for her sake.

Not that their marriage breakdown had been the only point at issue, she reminded herself wearily. Lionel's relationship with Gabriel had always been a volatile one. As father and son, apart from the shrewd business brains they shared, they had always been chalk and cheese.

They didn't even look alike. Lionel had been ruggedly built and fair-haired, with a florid complexion. Gabriel was equally tall, but his body was lean, like whipcord. And his dark, saturnine good looks were wholly derived from his Italian mother.

Temperamentally, they'd been poles apart too. Lionel had been bluff, outspoken and sentimental. A man who enjoyed life openly and always had a good word for his neighbours.

Gabriel, on the other hand...

Ah, she thought. What was Gabriel? Had she ever really known?

There were the surface attributes, of course. The quiet, rather drawling voice, the attractive, crooked smile, the athleticism, the raw courage he displayed on the polo field and riding in point-to-points, the icy nerve he brought to his business dealings. But none of these gave any real clue to what was going on in his mind.

He seemed, she thought, to watch the world from behind a screen of faint amusement. There'd always been a reserve, a control in his behaviour, even when he'd made love to her—after the first time, at least, she thought, her throat tightening harshly, and this had forced her, in turn, further behind her own barriers of shyness and tension.

Not that she could altogether blame him, she made herself concede. He hadn't wanted to marry her. The situation had been forced on him.

Lionel had just retired as chairman of Verne Investments and he'd needed Gabriel to succeed him, but only on his own terms.

Joanna had always been aware of their constant conflict over Gabriel's hedonistic lifestyle, the partying, the high-profile sport, the procession of spectacular girlfriends. The head of Verne Investments needed a more sober, stable image, Lionel had declared sternly. And becoming a married man would be the first step in his rehabilitation.

And I was there, Joanna thought bitterly. Already groomed for stardom, though I didn't know it. And with a stupid, schoolgirl crush on Gabriel that I conveniently mistook for the real thing.

And for Lionel it solved two problems at once—Gabriel's need for a suitable wife, and his own wish to see me provided for in the future.

No wonder he'd swept them into it, she thought painfully. His motives, as always, had been of the purest, but the pressure was there just the same. And Gabriel's ambition coupled with her own agonising *naïveté* had set the seal on the whole disaster.

She had been eighteen. He was ten years older. And from the day, four years earlier, when she'd gone to live at Westroe Manor, he'd been her god—a magical being who would suddenly arrive and turn her life to radiance.

He'd taught her to ride, played tennis with her, forcing her to improve her game, drunk her first champagne with her, swept her off to London to have her soft, straight brown hair properly cut, bolstered her uncertain dress sense and nursed her, straight-faced, through her first hangover.

He had also shielded her from Cynthia's occasional ill-tempered or patronising jibes, turning them aside with some cool, cutting rejoinder.

Looking back, Joanna thought that had probably had more to do with his dislike of Cynthia than any feeling of protectiveness towards herself. Yet at the time she'd seen him as her own white knight, riding to the rescue.

And she'd been too dazzled to realise that he was treating her just like the younger sister he'd never had.

Instead I thought I was Cinderella, she mocked herself, and that Gabriel was Prince Charming. And that Lionel, my fairy godfather, would somehow turn this cold-blooded business arrangement into a love-match, and we'd live happily ever after.

But her honeymoon in the Mauritian villa hired for them, had sent all her illusions crashing round her ears.

Beginning, she thought, hugging her arms defensively round her body, with her wedding night that wasn't.

At the time she'd thought he was just being considerate. That he'd realised the demands of the wedding and the subsequent long flight had exhausted her when he'd told her quietly to go to bed and get some sleep, while he used an adjoining room. She'd even been grateful.

They'd spent the following day quietly at the villa, relaxing at the side of the pool under sunshades. But when evening came, Joanna had been able to feel tension beginning to build inside her.

She'd mentally told herself off for being an idiot.

She knew what the mechanics of sex entailed, of course, but nothing of the sweeping emotions that transformed it into love.

They'd had a late and lingering dinner on the verandah overlooking the garden. Joanna had refused the brandy Gabriel offered her with their coffee, and instantly regretted it. Maybe it would have dispelled the colony of butterflies which had taken up residence inside her.

Gabriel, too, had been quiet over their meal, and was sitting, staring into the velvety darkness, cradling his glass in one hand.

For a moment she'd wondered if he was nervous too, then dismissed the idea. Gabriel, after all, was hardly a novice in these matters, she'd told herself, swallowing.

At last, she'd pushed back her chair. 'I—I think I'll go to bed,' she said.

'Fine.' His smile was abstracted, as if his thoughts were far away.

'Are you going to stay here?' Her voice quivered a little.

He turned his head slowly and looked at her. He was frowning slightly, and there was a faint hardness about the lines of his mouth.

He said quietly, 'For a while—yes.'

Her throat seemed to have closed up, making speech impossible, so she made herself smile and nod, then escaped to her room.

She showered, and put on the nightgown bought specially for this momentous occasion—crisp and delicate in white broderie anglaise—then slid under the sheet which was the bed's only covering to wait for Gabriel.

The minutes ticked by—became half an hour—and

then an hour. In spite of herself, Joanna could feel her eyelids becoming heavy, her body sinking down into the mattress.

No, she thought, sitting up. I'm not going to sleep.

She allowed another fifteen minutes to pass, then left the bed and padded barefoot to the door. The passage outside was in darkness, but she could see a glimmer of light shining under the door of the next room.

Swallowing, she turned the handle and walked in.

Gabriel was in bed, reading, propped up by a mountain of pillows, the sheet pulled to cover his hips, his olive skin in dark contrast to the whiteness of the linen.

Something clenched inside her at the sight of him. Something alien—dangerous—exciting.

There was a ring on her hand telling her that she was his wife. But he seemed in no hurry to be her husband.

His smile was edged, almost wary as he looked at her. 'What is it, Jo?'

'I—I wondered where you were.'

'Not very far away, as you see.'

'Yes.' The drum of her heartbeat was almost painful. 'But why here?'

He said gently, 'It's late. Let's talk tomorrow.'

She walked forward and stood beside the bed, her eyes fixed on him as if she was seeing him for the first time, observing the strength of bone and muscle beneath the smooth skin. The way the shadowing of body hair on his chest narrowed to a vee over his abdomen. And, she realised, how he'd positioned the book he was holding to conceal the fact that he was physically aroused.

'Go to bed, Jo.' There was a snap in his voice.

She reached out and touched his bare shoulder, feeling the muscles bunch under her fingers.

She said softly, 'Won't you kiss me goodnight first?'

And she leaned forward and put her mouth on his, softly, almost experimentally.

For a moment he was completely still, then, with a sound like a groan, his arms went round her, pulling her roughly down to him so that she was cradled across his body.

His lips were parting hers without any of the usual gentleness he showed her. She felt the graze of his teeth against her bottom lip, the heated thrust of his tongue.

Excitement warred with apprehension inside her.

Gabriel tossed the covering sheet away and lowered her to the mattress, kneeling over her. He took the hem of her nightdress, tugging the garment upwards and over her head, then throwing it aside.

She wasn't used to being naked in front of anyone, and she was paralysed with shyness. She wanted Gabriel to hold her. To kiss her and reassure her. She wanted him to tell her he loved her.

But he did none of these things. Instead, he began to touch her, his hands shaking as they cupped her breasts, traced the curve of her stomach and swept downwards to her thighs.

Joanna felt a faint stir of wondering response deep within her. She looked up at him and suddenly saw the face of a stranger, harsh and strangely remote, with eyes feral as a jungle cat's. As he entered her, her body resisted momentarily the breach of its innocence, and she gave a sob of mingled pain and fright.

He checked suddenly, looking down at her with

something like horror.. He whispered harshly, 'Oh, dear God...'

Then he began to move inside her, to some stark, driven rhythm of his own, until, at last, his release was torn from him.

He rolled away from her and lay with his back turned to her while his ragged breathing steadied. Then he got up and went into the bathroom, and she heard the shower running.

A ritual cleansing, Joanna thought, to wash away all contact with her. And she turned her face into the pillow and wept.

She supposed she must have cried herself to sleep, because the next time she opened her eyes it was sunrise. She was alone in the bedroom, but she could see Gabriel sitting on the balcony, in his robe, watching the sun come up, a dark silhouette against the passionate sky.

She slipped out of bed, put on the crumpled nightgown rescued from the floor and went to him.

'Gabriel.' Her voice barely rose above a whisper, and she saw his back stiffen in awareness.

'Go back to bed.' He didn't look round at her. 'You'll catch cold.'

'I don't understand.' She forced the words through a throat aching with tears. 'What have I done wrong?'

'Nothing,' he said quietly. 'The fault is all mine. I should have stopped this bloody marriage at the outset—never allowed it to happen.' His sigh was harsh, almost anguished. 'Dear God, what a mess. What a total—damnable shambles.'

It was as if he'd turned and struck her. She went back into the bedroom, pulled the sheet over her head, and lay like a stone until the servants started moving about.

And then she got up quietly, to pull the remnants of her pride around her and face the first day of the rest of her life.

CHAPTER TWO

JOANNA stirred in the chair and shivered. The hopeful fire had burned down, and she replenished it with a couple of fast-burning beech logs.

But the real cold was inside her, in her bones. In her heart.

She shook her head in irritation. Why was she thinking these things—allowing herself to remember—probing into old wounds?

Perhaps, she thought, grimacing, because they'd never properly healed the first time. Now there's a dangerous admission.

Wrapping her arms across herself, she began to walk slowly up and down the room, head bent. Her hair brushed her cheek and she combed it back with impatient fingers. She was still wearing it in the same sleek mid-length bob. A change, she decided abruptly, was well overdue.

Something short, she thought, and businesslike, befitting her job-seeking status.

She had filled in for the secretary more than once at the estate office, so she knew the rudiments of word-processing and the preparation of spreadsheets.

What she should look for, she thought detachedly, was a position similar to the one she'd filled here, but minus the personal involvement. Housekeepers who could drive and had basic secretarial skills would surely be in demand. And didn't the National Trust employ people to live in their properties and care for them?

I would like to do that, she thought. I would like to care for the fabric of another old house, as I've looked after this. It'll be handed back to Gabriel in good shape.

She had marked time for the past two years, but if that led to a career then the time would have been well spent after all. It was only a pity she couldn't find a suitable post before she was forced to confront Gabriel again.

Gabriel. Every pathway in her mind seemed suddenly to lead back to him, she thought angrily. But that was understandable, in a way. After all, in another forty-eight hours he would be here, taking possession.

Another uncontrollable shiver went through her as the words lodged in her brain. For a brief nightmare second she could almost feel his physical presence. She could feel his hands touching her, as if she were some rare and delicate object which had taken his fleeting interest but which he would decide, in the end, not to buy. Her head seemed to fill with the scent—the taste of him.

And she remembered his face, stark, almost pagan in the golden Mauritian moonlight, as he'd lifted himself above her. The way he'd suddenly become some fierce, dominating stranger, obsessed with an emotion she did not share or even understand.

But he had never treated her like that again.

Nor had either of them referred to what had happened, or the bitter words which had followed. Instead, by some tacit agreement, they'd treated the honeymoon as if it was just another holiday. They'd swum, gone sightseeing, bargain-hunted in local markets and sampled the Mauritian specialities in the restaurants like all the other tourists.

In the daytime, he'd seemed to revert to the Gabriel

she'd always known, so that she'd been able to relax, even enjoy herself a little. Except that she'd known the night would always come and she would find herself lying alone in the enormous bed, listening to the gentle swish of the ceiling fan as it revolved above her and wondering if he was asleep.

It was their last night on the island when he'd eventually turned to her again.

This time he'd been gentle, almost objective as he'd touched her. There'd been no pain when he entered her, but she'd been rigid in his arms, wanting to respond—longing to share this ultimate secret with him—but not daring to. Because she'd known from his own words that it was a mistake—that he didn't really want her. He needed sexual release and she was just an available female body. And that knowledge had imprisoned her in a constraint that this polite, controlled, *dutiful* coupling could not release.

At one point, she'd heard him ask quietly, 'Do you want me to stop?'

And her own stilted reply. 'No, it's all right—really.'

For a moment he'd been very still, staring down at her, then he'd closed his eyes and begun to drive towards his climax.

In a way things had become easier when they returned home. For one thing they hadn't been in each other's undiluted company any more.

But there had been inherent problems in the situation—Cynthia's almost prurient interest in their relationship for one, and Lionel's jovial hints about grandchildren for another.

If they'd been in love, passionately and physically involved with each other, they could have laughed about it. As it was, Joanna had found it acutely embarrassing. What Gabriel thought he'd kept to himself.

He had begun to stay overnight in London instead of driving down, and she'd had to find excuses not to join him.

When he was there, in bed with her in the room they'd shared for form's sake, she'd lie awake half the night, dreading he was going to touch her, then fretting because he'd simply wished her goodnight, turned on his side and instantly fallen asleep.

When he wasn't there, the darkness she'd stared into had been filled with images of him, the challenging grace of his naked body arched above some other woman.

And there had to be someone. Painful common sense had told her that. Gabriel was not a natural celibate, and the spaces between their lovemaking—if it could be called that—were becoming longer.

She remembered the very last time with painful vividness. They'd been to a party—someone's twenty-first birthday—and she'd drunk too much champagne. For once Joanna had felt her inhibitions slipping away. She'd laughed, flirted, and danced with everyone, suddenly aware as she did so that Gabriel was watching her, leaning against a wall, drink in hand. For a moment, she'd faltered, bracing herself for his disapproval, then realised that he was smiling faintly, his eyes hooded, speculative. She'd laughed back at him, and, obeying an impulse, spun around on the ball of her foot so that the skirt of her indigo crêpe dress billowed round her slim legs, blowing him a kiss as she faced him again. And she'd seen him, in return, lift his glass in a silent toast.

In the car going home, she'd kicked off her high-heeled shoes and slid down in her seat, allowing her head to droop towards his shoulder.

She'd half expected him to move away, but he'd stayed where he was and so had she, watching the passing hedgerows through half-closed eyes, moving her cheek gently against the smooth silky texture of his jacket, and humming snatches of the music she'd been dancing to.

They hadn't talked, but that in itself had imposed a kind of intimacy, as if there was no need for words.

Or, she'd thought afterwards, as if they had been in a dream.

When they'd got back to the Manor, Gabriel had parked by the front entrance and come round to open Joanna's door. She'd been scrabbling around on the floor.

'I've lost my shoe.'

'Look for it tomorrow.'

'But the gravel—' She stopped abruptly as he lifted her out of the car into his arms, and carried her up the short flight of stone steps into the house.

She expected him to set her down in the hall, but he kept going up the stairs, then along the gallery to their bedroom.

She could feel her heart hammering suddenly. The effect of the champagne had dissipated and she was sober again, half-frightened, half-excited.

Gabriel carried her across the room and put her on the bed, following her down onto the yielding mattress. For a moment he lay beside her, one hand cupping her face, making her look at him. His eyes were lambent, intent, as if, she thought, he was looking into her soul. The silence that surrounded them was charged. The light from the shaded lamps seemed to shimmer and dance.

Joanna was trembling inside, almost dizzy with expectancy. She lifted her own hand and stroked his cheek lightly with her fingertips, and she saw him hesitate, the lean body suddenly tense, the dark face unfathomable.

And she remembered, just in time, as he must also have done, the bitter truth about their marriage, and that to yield to the sweet, potent forces in her blood—to draw him down into her arms—into her body—would be an unendurable complication.

Because nothing's basically changed, she thought, her throat tightening. He's had a good time at the party tonight and he wants to end the evening in the traditional way. That's all.

And I—I can't let myself want him. I couldn't bear to be hurt like that—to spend the rest of my life waiting for him, needing him, and being disappointed. Being betrayed.

It's better the way it is. At least I still have my pride.

She moved abruptly, pushing herself away from him.

He reached for her. 'Joanna.' His voice was gentle, almost rueful.

She said in a small, high voice, 'I—I'm sorry. I'm not feeling very well.'

She slid off the bed, a hand pressed to her mouth, and ran across to the bathroom, closing the door and bolting it behind her.

It wasn't altogether a lie. She felt sick with self-betrayal.

She ran the taps in the basin and splashed water onto her face and wrists. After a decent interval she flushed the lavatory and emerged from the bathroom, dabbing her lips with a tissue.

Gabriel, still fully dressed, was standing by the window, looking out into the darkness. He turned, brows raised, and surveyed her.

Joanna gave him a tremulous smile. 'That was awful. It must have been the champagne.'

'Naturally,' he said. 'There's nothing else, after all, that could have turned your stomach.'

She halted uncomfortably, disturbed by his unwavering scrutiny.

'I hope you've never had leanings towards becoming an actress,' he went on conversationally. 'You're not very good at it.'

She felt colour invade her face. 'I—I don't know what you're talking about.'

'Your recent performance as the dying swan,' he said derisively. 'But you won't have to sink to any more of these undignified ploys to keep me at bay. Enough is quite enough.'

He paused, the tawny eyes sweeping her contemptuously. 'I think I'll do us both a favour, and find some other form of entertainment.'

He walked past her to the door. 'I'm going back to London. You can tell my father I had an early meeting, or make up what story you like. It really makes no difference.' His smile flickered at her like a cold flame. 'Goodbye, my sweet wife.'

Joanna realised dazedly that she was standing in the middle of the study with her eyes shut and her hands pressed tightly to her ears, as if—two years on—she could somehow shut out the sound, the image of that night, and by doing so reduce its pain.

But that, she reminded herself bleakly, had never been possible. And with Gabriel's return it would all begin again. The day after tomorrow, Henry Fortescue had said. Forty-eight hours, maybe less, and she would have to face him.

Yes—on the positive side—forty-eight hours and the official dissolution of their marriage could begin.

She would leave the letter she had written him on the desk for him to find.

She took a long look around her. The chances were she would never enter this room again. The house that had been her home was hers no longer.

I have to move out, she thought. Move out—and move on.

And, whatever emotional furore Gabriel's return would cause, there were still practical details to be dealt with.

She went out of the study, crossing the big panelled hall to the dining room, where Mrs Ashby was laying the table for dinner.

The housekeeper's elderly face was drawn, her eyes red-rimmed. Joanna remembered with compassion that she had lived at Westroe in one capacity or another for over thirty years, arriving when Gabriel was still a baby.

The smile she sent Joanna was a travesty of her usual cheerfulness. 'Will Mrs Elcott be down for dinner, madam? Or should I prepare a tray?'

'I honestly don't know, but I'll find out.' Joanna paused. 'Mr Verne will be here for the funeral, Grace. Would you get a room ready for him, please?'

Grace Ashby shook her head. 'What a sad home-coming for him, madam.' She hesitated awkwardly. 'I suppose it should be Mr Lionel's room, but all his things are still there. I—I haven't had the heart to touch anything, and that's a fact.'

'Just prepare the room he used to have for the time being,' Joanna said gently. 'He can decide for himself

what he wants to do once things—settle down a bit.'
She sighed. 'Now, I'll go and tackle Mrs Elcott.'

The lamps had been lit in Cynthia's bedroom, and
she was reclining against her pillows in a pale blue
wrap, watching television. A copy of *Vogue* was open
on the bed beside her, together with a half-eaten box
of chocolates.

'Hi.' Joanna smiled at her, trying not to wince at
the over-heated, perfume-laden atmosphere. 'How are
you feeling? I came to see if you felt like coming
down to dinner this evening.'

'I'll have a bowl of soup up here.' Cynthia gave
her a tragic look. 'I'm afraid I can't face anything
more solid.'

And nor could I if I'd eaten my way through nearly
a pound of chocolates, Joanna thought with irony.

Aloud, she said, 'I'm sorry to hear that.'

'It's not your fault.' Cynthia waved a hand. 'Some
of us are just more sensitive than others. It's the bur-
den we have to bear in life.'

She thought of another one. 'And how many more
visitors can we expect today?' she demanded peevish-
ly. 'The doorbell seems to have been ringing non-
stop. It's been quite impossible for me to rest.'

'It's natural for people to express their condolences,' Joanna said levelly. 'Lionel was very much
loved.'

'You think you have to tell me that?' Cynthia
snatched a handful of tissues from a box and applied
them to her perfectly dry eyes. 'Really, Joanna, you
can be so tactless. I sometimes wonder if you have a
heart at all.' She paused. 'I notice none of them came
up to see me. I suppose I can expect to be disregarded
from now on.' She sighed. 'And things might have
been so different.'

'They're going to be.' Joanna cleared a handful of lingerie and filmy stockings from a chair and sat down. 'My last visitor was Henry Fortescue.'

'Old Fortescue?' Cynthia sat up abruptly, her wrap slipping from her shoulder. 'Did he mention Lionel's will, by any chance? Give a hint how things had been left?'

Joanna was used to her stepmother by now, but there were still moments when Cynthia's capacity for self-interest left her stunned.

'No,' she returned tautly. 'The will's going to be read after the funeral.' She swallowed. 'When Gabriel is here.'

'Of course.' Cynthia gave a slow, sly smile. 'The return of the prodigal heir. No wonder you're so edgy.'

Joanna was about to retort irritably that she wasn't edgy at all, but stopped herself just in time.

'How do you feel about seeing him again?' Cynthia helped herself to another chocolate. 'And, more importantly, how's he going to feel about seeing you? He must blame you for the fact that he hasn't been near the place for two years.' She began to roll the paper wrapping into a tiny ball. 'After all, he hasn't just been separated from you, but from his father as well, and now the separation's permanent.'

'You don't have to remind me of that,' Joanna said bleakly. 'I should have been the one to go.'

'Oh, don't be a. fool,' Cynthia said impatiently. 'Lionel would never have allowed that.' She examined a fleck on her nail. 'You do realise he was madly in love with your mother, don't you?'

Joanna stared at her in silent shock. 'What are you talking about?' she asked eventually.

'Your father told me all about it.' Cynthia shrugged

nonchalantly. 'It was one of those boy-girl things, and the families discouraged it because they were first cousins, but Jeremy reckoned he carried a torch for her all his life.' She gave Joanna a sidelong smile. 'Why do you think I brought you here after your father was killed? I knew all I had to do was tug a few heartstrings and we'd have a home for life.'

'I think that had more to do with Lionel's strong sense of family than any secret passion,' Joanna said dismissively. 'You're surely not suggesting he married Valentina on some kind of rebound?'

Cynthia shrugged again, giving an irritable hitch to her slipping wrap. 'God knows why he married her, because of all the ill-matched couples...' She pursed her lips. 'Can you imagine? A Roman beauty, descended from centuries of aristocratic decadence, buried alive in the English countryside. She must have thought she'd died and gone to hell.'

'And yet they stayed together,' Joanna objected.

'By the skin of their teeth.' Cynthia yawned, and ate another chocolate. 'Jeremy told me they used to have the most spectacular rows—real plate-throwing, screaming jobs. You can see why Gabriel's no angel, in spite of his name.'

She paused, her expression soulful. 'I think that is why poor Lionel was so scared of actual commitment for a second time. If only we'd had more time together, I might have been able to reassure him.'

At the same time keeping a close watch for flying pigs, Joanna thought drily.

Whatever her stepmother's ego might suggest, Joanna herself had never seen in Lionel's behaviour towards Cynthia anything more than a rather studied courtesy. On the other hand, the full-length portrait of his late wife still occupied pride of place on the wall of the Jacobean Room, with its big carved four-poster bed, which they'd shared during their marriage and he'd occupied until his own death.

Cynthia directed a malicious look at her. 'Did Gabriel ever bung any plates in your direction? No, I suppose he was far too civilised—although I often thought there was something pretty volcanic seething under that calm exterior.'

Joanna's lips tightened in distaste. 'I wouldn't know.'

Cynthia laughed. 'Oh, I'm quite sure of that, darling. Another marriage from hell,' she added reflectively. 'Gabriel must have cursed the day he allowed himself to be manoeuvred into it.'

'Probably.' Joanna got to her feet. 'And soon you'll have every opportunity to ask him about it. Although I doubt if he'll tell you.'

'I wouldn't be too certain about that.' Cynthia stretched like a cat in the big bed. 'There's less than six years' difference in our ages, you know. He might welcome—a confidante.'

There was something in her voice that stopped Joanna in her tracks.

'What exactly are you saying?' she asked slowly. 'That having failed with the father you're going after the son?'

Cynthia's blue eyes took on a steely glint. 'Crudely put, my sweet, but not altogether inaccurate,' she retorted. 'God knows, I've got to do something. Unlike you, I can't count on Lionel's will to rescue me. If we'd been officially engaged it would have been very different, of course. I might have had some claim. Although I'm pretty certain he's left me Larkspur Cottage. Certainly I dropped enough hints.'

She paused. 'And why should you quibble, anyway? You don't want Gabriel, so why be a dog in the manger?'

'I wouldn't dream of it.' Joanna had a feeling of total unreality. 'And please don't let the fact that we're still married to each other stand in your way either.'

'No, I shan't,' Cynthia returned. 'And neither, I suspect, will Gabriel.'

It was all Joanna could do not to bang the bedroom door as she left.

Her heart was hammering, and she felt oddly nauseous as she went into her own room to change for dinner.

Gabriel and Cynthia, she thought. Cynthia and Gabriel.

Could such a relationship exist in the realms of possibility?

She swallowed past the sudden constriction in her throat, trying to think dispassionately about her stepmother as she reached into the wardrobe and extracted a woollen long-sleeved blouse and a plain black skirt.

Cynthia was thirty-seven against Gabriel's thirty-two, she thought, but she didn't look her age. She never had. She was a regular patron of the nearby health farm, using the gym almost as much as the beauty salon. She played tennis in the summer, squash in the winter, and golf all the year round. Her clothes and make-up were always immaculate, and her blond hair skilfully highlighted.

Superficially, at least, she was a far more obvious and decorative chatelaine for the Manor than Joanna had ever been—or ever could be, she thought, giving her straight brown hair, pale skin and clear hazel eyes a disparaging glance in the mirror.

And Cynthia was undoubtedly a man's woman. She

wasn't simply attractive, she had a deep, inbuilt sex appeal that announced itself in her voice, her body language and mannerisms whenever she was in male company.

Lionel might have been resistant to her allure, but he'd been an exception. Joanna had seen sensible, responsible men become quite silly when Cynthia turned her honeyed charm on them.

My own father, for one, she thought sadly.

From the first, Cynthia had pursued Lionel quite single-mindedly. But what would have happened if she'd made Gabriel the object of her attentions instead? Lionel might not have approved, but would he really have raised any serious opposition to their marriage—if that had been what they both wanted?

Gabriel never wanted me, she thought. So why not Cynthia?

I'm divorcing him, so what can it possibly matter who he chooses—the second time around?

And then she saw the sudden flare of colour along her cheekbones, felt the angry knock of her heart against her ribcage and the burn of anger in her eyes.

And she knew that beyond all logic and reason, and without any doubt, it mattered a great deal.

A realisation which terrified her.

CHAPTER THREE

DINNER was a sombre and solitary affair. Joanna drank the vegetable soup and picked at the grilled chicken breast, conscious all the time of the empty chair at the head of the table.

Jess and Molly, Lionel's two retrievers, lay dejectedly in the doorway, silky golden heads pillowed in bewilderment on their paws.

'Poor old girls.' She bent to give them each a consolatory pat as she left the room. 'No one's been taking much notice of you, and you don't understand any of it. Never mind, I'll take you both up on the hill later.'

She drank her coffee by the drawing room fire, the dogs stretched on the rug at her feet. The morning paper lay on the table beside her, still neatly folded. Usually she and Lionel would have been arguing companionably over the crossword by now, she thought, with a pang of desolation.

She drew a sharp breath. 'I've got to stop looking back,' she whispered fiercely to herself. 'Because that brings nothing but pain.'

The future was something she dared not contemplate. Which left only the emptiness of the present.

She knew she would deal with that unwelcome moment of revelation she'd experienced before dinner. It was essential to rationalise and somehow dismiss it before Gabriel came back.

I'm in an emotional low, she told herself. I'm

bound to be vulnerable—prey to all kinds of ridiculous imaginings.

Or maybe Cynthia's right, and I'm just a dog in the manger.

I could live with that, she thought. But not with the possibility that Gabriel is still of importance in my life.

Determinedly, and deliberately, she switched her attention to another of Cynthia's bombshells—that Lionel had been affected his whole life through by his passion for Joanna's mother. Could it be true? she wondered.

Certainly she'd never heard him say anything that gave credence to such an idea. However tempestuous his marriage had been, she'd always believed that he'd loved Valentina Alessio. And he had never seriously contemplated putting another woman in her place—whatever Cynthia might choose to think.

Henry Fortescue had described Mary Verne as Lionel's favourite cousin, and that was how she still planned to regard their relationship.

A low whine from one of the dogs reminded her that she'd promised to take them out.

She pulled on some boots, shrugged on her waxed jacket, and wound a scarf round her neck.

She collected a flashlight and let herself out by the side door, the dogs capering joyfully round her. They went through the garden, across the field, and onto the hill via the rickety wooden stile.

The temperature had fallen, and a damp, icy wind was blowing, making Joanna shiver in spite of her jacket.

Cold enough for snow, she thought as she followed the gambolling dogs up the well-worn track.

'Don't get too excited,' she warned them. 'We'll go as far as the Hermitage and then I'm turning back.'

It was a stiff climb, and the ground was slippery and treacherous with loose stones. She was breathless when she reached the awkward huddle of rocks on the summit, and quite glad to lean her back against the largest boulder and shelter from the penetrating wind.

The dogs were hurtling about in the dead bracken, yelping excitedly. Joanna clicked off the flashlight to save the battery, and shoved it in her pocket.

It was a good spot for star-gazing, but tonight the sky was busy with scudding clouds.

Joanna looked back the way she had come. The Manor lay below her in the valley. There was a light in the kitchen wing, and one from Cynthia's bedroom, but the rest of the house was in darkness.

A week ago it would have been ablaze with lights. Lionel had liked brightness and warmth, and had never mastered the theory that electricity switches operated in an 'off' position too.

The blank windows said more plainly than anything else that the master was no longer at home.

The wind mourned softly among the fallen stones. Local legend said that centuries before a man had come to this place and built himself a stone shelter where he could pray and do penance for his sins in complete solitude, and that the keening of the wind was the hermit weeping for his past wickedness.

And so would I, thought Joanna, adjusting her scarf more securely. She called the dogs and they came trotting to her side. As she reached for her torch they stiffened, and she heard them growl softly.

'Easy,' she told them. 'It's only a sheep—or a deer.'

They were too well-behaved to go chasing live-

stock, but something had clearly spooked them. Or
someone, Joanna thought with sudden alarm, as she
heard the rattle of a stray pebble nearby. Her fingers
tightened around the unlit torch. Normally she'd expect to have the hill to herself on a night like this.

Perhaps it was the hermit, who was said to wander
across the top of the hill in robe and cowl, usually
when the moon was full, she thought, her mouth twisting in self-derision.

She said clearly, 'Jess—Moll—it's all right.'

For a moment they were still under her restraining
hand, then with a whimper of excitement they leapt
forward into the darkness. A moment later she heard
them barking hysterically a short distance away.

'Damnation.' She switched on the torch and followed them, cursing herself for not having brought
their leashes.

She could only hope they hadn't flushed some
hardy courting couple out of the bracken.

She could see their quarry now, a tall, dark figure,
standing quietly while the dogs leapt about him, yelping in joyous welcome.

She hurried into speech. 'Good evening. I do hope
they're not annoying you. They're not usually like this
with strangers.'

For a moment he neither moved nor spoke, then he
put down a hand and the dogs sank to their haunches,
their faces lifted worshipfully towards him.

And Joanna knew in that instant, with a sudden sick
dread, exactly who was standing in front of her in the
darkness.

He said quietly, 'They're not annoying me, Joanna.
And I'm hardly a stranger.'

The breath caught in her throat. She took a quick

step backwards, the torch swinging up to illumine his face and confirm her worst fear.

Her voice was a scratchy whisper. 'Gabriel?'

'Congratulations. You have an excellent memory.'

She disregarded the jibe. 'What are you doing here?'

'My father died yesterday.' A harshness invaded the usually cool drawl. 'I've come to attend his funeral.'

'But we weren't expecting you—not for another two days.'

'I decided to end my self-imposed exile and take an earlier flight. I hope it won't cause you too much inconvenience.'

She swallowed. 'No—no, of course not.'

'Said with no conviction at all,' he murmured. 'Not that it makes a ha'p'orth of difference. I'm here, and I intend to spend the night under my own roof. And if that's a problem for you, Joanna, you're just going to have to sort it out.'

She said tautly, 'You're forty-eight hours early, that's all. No big deal. And if anyone's going to be inconvenienced it will be Mrs Ashby. I'd better go down and warn her.' She paused. 'Moll—Jess—come on.'

The retrievers didn't budge. Gabriel laughed softly. 'They seemed to have transferred their allegiance.'

She said, 'Like all good subjects at the start of a new reign.'

'Is that how you see yourself too?' There was faint amusement in his voice. 'Can I expect the same unquestioning obedience?'

She said shortly, 'You can expect nothing,' and plunged off down the path, aware that her face had warmed.

Don't you ever learn? she castigated herself. Why bandy words with him when you always lose? Don't let him wind you up.

He caught up with her easily, the dogs pacing at his heels. 'Take it easy. You might fall.'

And break my neck? she thought bitterly. I'm not that lucky.

She said, 'What were you doing up there anyway?'

'I've spent the past twenty-four hours cooped up in boardrooms and shut in a plane,' he returned shortly. 'I needed to breathe—and to think.'

And to grieve, she realised, with sudden remorse.

She said haltingly, 'I—I'm sorry I intruded.'

'Where else would you take the dogs?' His tone was dismissive.

They continued on downhill. Even with the torch-light to guide her, Joanna found the slope hard going. She was burdened by her awareness of Gabriel walking beside her, close enough to touch, but not touching—inhibited by her fear that if she put a foot wrong he would reach out a hand to her, and that invisible, necessary barrier would be shattered.

She needed to say something—to break the silence. 'You might have telephoned,' she remarked. 'Told us to expect you.'

He said lightly, 'I decided against it. You might have changed the locks.'

'That isn't very amusing.' Her tone was chilly.

'Who said I was joking?' He paused, then said more gently, 'Look, forget I said that. I suspect this is going to be a bloody difficult few days, Jo. Let's do what we can to preserve the outward decencies, whatever our private feelings. For Lionel's sake.'

'You don't have to bludgeon me with his memory,' she said raggedly. 'I'll behave.' She drew a breath.

'I'll go on ahead, give Mrs Ashby a hand. Have you had dinner?'

'I had something on the plane. It successfully destroyed my appetite for the foreseeable future.'

'Oh.' She hesitated. 'Well, when you bring the dogs in, will you dry off their paws, please? You'll find their towels—'

'In the rear cloakroom,' he supplied. 'Where they've always been. I've been gone for two years, Joanna. It's hardly a lifetime.'

She bit her lip. 'I thought it might have slipped your memory, that's all.'

'Oh, no, Joanna.' His voice was quiet, almost reflective. 'I think I can safely promise you that I haven't forgotten a thing. Not the smallest detail.'

In the brief silence which followed, her sharply indrawn breath was clearly audible.

He nodded, as if satisfied, then added, 'Now, go and break the good news to Mrs Ashby. Like the dogs, she'll be pleased to see me.'

Joanna turned and, half-stumbling, half-running, made her way back to the house.

Mrs Ashby's reaction to the news was all Gabriel could have wished. She shed a few tears, smiled through them, made a few disjointed remarks, and bustled off to prepare his room.

Joanna knew she should have offered to help, but as she couldn't in honesty share the good woman's raptures she decided to keep her distance.

He's been back five minutes, she thought, and he's managed to unnerve me already. By the end of the week I'll be a basket case.

When Gabriel himself returned, she was sitting in the drawing room, having dragged together the threads of her composure. She'd discarded her jacket and boots but resisted the impulse to tidy her wind-blown hair, or disguise the pallor of her face with cosmetics.

'Well, this is a cosy, domestic scene.'

Joanna glanced up from the book she'd snatched up at random, and was pretending to read, to find him lounging in the doorway, watching her, his eyes hooded, his face inscrutable.

'It's better than you realise,' she returned, trying to sound casual, in spite of the sudden dryness in her throat. 'Grace has brought in a tray of fresh coffee. May I pour some for you?'

'No, don't get up. I'll do it.' He walked over to the side table and busied himself with the cafetière and cream jug. 'She wanted to serve up a fatted calf, but I persuaded her just coffee would be fine.'

To her annoyance, the cup he handed her was just as she liked it. His memory for detail was indeed disturbingly good, she reflected uneasily.

Gabriel looked down at the book she was holding and whistled appreciatively.

'Wisden? Is this interest in cricketing statistics a new departure?'

'Not particularly.' Joanna flushed with annoyance. Of all the damned things she could have chosen, she thought angrily. She closed the book with a bang, and put it down. 'Actually, I began watching the game to keep your father company.'

His smile was tight-lipped. 'Of course,' he drawled. 'The perfect daughter.' He paused, then added softly, 'In-law.'

'Thank you,' she said. 'I think.'

He seated himself opposite her on one of the big chintz-covered sofas which flanked the fireplace. The dogs, who'd followed him into the room, lay down on the rug between them.

For the first time Joanna was able to take a real look at him, studying him covertly from under her lashes.

He'd changed, she thought. The lines beside his mouth had deepened, and his features had lost any last trace of boyishness. He looked not just older, but harder.

He glanced up, meeting her gaze meditatively, and she hurried into speech.

'You were a long time coming down from the hill.'

His brows lifted. 'Did you miss me?' he drawled. 'I'm flattered.'

She bit her lip. 'That isn't what I meant.'

His mouth twisted. 'I didn't really think it would be.' He drank some coffee. 'I went down the other way—to pick up my car. I'd left it in the lay-by at Combe Gate.'

'Oh,' Joanna said rather blankly. 'I see.'

'No,' he said gently. 'I don't think you do. I wasn't sure in my own mind whether I was ready to come back to this house yet, or if I preferred to spend the night in Midhampton. I went up onto the hill to spy out the lie of the land, and then you came along and the dogs recognised me. That seemed to make the decision for me.'

She said slowly, 'If I'd been alone would you have said anything? Let me know you were there?'

'Ah,' he said lightly. 'That we shall never know.'

'Well—I think your decision was the right one.' She paused. 'Your room will be ready by now. I—I expect after all that travelling you'd appreciate an early night.'

'Not particularly,' he said. 'I think, don't you, that we should talk? Settle a few things?'

'Yes,' she said, her heart sinking. 'Perhaps you're right.' She drew a deep breath. 'Gabriel, you may not want to hear this from me, but I really loved your father, and I—I'm devastated by what's happened.'

He stared down at the cup and saucer he was holding. 'Well, at least we agree on something.'

'I had no idea he had any kind of heart trouble.'

Gabriel shrugged a shoulder. 'I presume he didn't want to worry you.'

She stared at him. 'Then—you knew?' she asked incredulously.

'Yes.' His voice was even. His tawny gaze met hers in direct challenge. 'I've been seeing him quite regularly in London. The last time was a couple of weeks ago, when he came up to consult a specialist who recommended a by-pass operation.' He paused. 'But unfortunately fate intervened.'

He gave her a speculative look. 'Our meetings have clearly come as an unpleasant shock to you. If you'd hoped the breach between us was total, and I'd be cut off with the proverbial shilling, you're going to be disappointed.'

She stood up, spilling coffee down her skirt. 'How dare you say that?' Her voice shook. 'I never thought—never wanted you to be apart from him. I've been blaming myself terribly...'

'And scalding yourself as penance, it seems,' Gabriel said grimly. 'Are you hurt?'

'No, of course not.' She dabbed crossly at her damp skirt with a hankie. 'God, how stupid.'

'Sit down,' he said more gently. 'And calm down.'

'I was perfectly calm,' she said, off the edge of her voice, 'until you started your—rotten insinuations.'

'Mea culpa.' His tone was almost casual. 'Consider yourself absolved—of that particular crime anyway. And don't throw any more coffee about,' he added, as her head lifted in shock and she glared at him.

'Is this your idea of preserving the decencies?' she demanded.

'That's in public,' he said. 'This is private—just between the two of us. Husband to wife.'

'Is that how you still regard us?' Joanna perched tensely on the edge of the sofa.

He shrugged. 'It happens to remain a legal reality, however regrettable.'

'But not for much longer.' Joanna swallowed. 'Gabriel, we married each other for all the wrong reasons, but it doesn't have to be a life sentence. Not any more.'

'What do you suggest?'

'A quick divorce,' she said. 'Then we can both get on with our lives.' She paused. 'Actually, I—I wrote you a letter with my proposals. It's on the desk in the study.'

'How very efficient of you,' he said slowly. 'You certainly didn't waste any time.'

'It seemed to me we'd wasted enough already.' She forced a smile. 'And there's nothing—no one—to keep us together any more.'

He said coldly. 'I do not need to be reminded of that, thank you.'

She winced. 'I'm sorry. But you know it's true.' She drew a deep breath. 'We married each other because it was what Lionel wanted, and we made a wretched mess of it all.' She hesitated. 'I think he regretted it too.'

'I know he did.' Gabriel's tone was dry.

'Well, then,' she prompted.

He got up and went over to the table to pour himself some more coffee.

'I don't think we should file for divorce before the funeral,' he said, without turning. 'It might look rather pointed.'

She stiffened. 'I wasn't suggesting that. And it's not a joke.'

'Bloody right, it isn't,' he said with sudden violence, and she jumped.

'You were the one who wanted to talk,' she said defensively.

'I did not, however, choose this particular topic of conversation,' he retorted, returning to his seat. 'Maybe we should postpone it until we're both feeling a little less raw.'

Her voice was uncertain. 'But you said there were things to settle.'

'About the funeral, mainly.' His firm lips tightened. 'One of the reasons I came back today was so that you wouldn't have to handle things all by yourself.'

'That was thoughtful of you,' she said stiffly. 'I made a list this morning of everything there was to do. Perhaps you'd better look through it and see what I've forgotten.'

'I don't think I dare,' he murmured.

'Gabriel—this isn't easy for me. Lionel wasn't just my father-in-law. He was my dearest friend. Whatever our personal feelings, we should—respect his memory and try to work together.'

'That's a good speech,' he approved. 'Did you think of it all by yourself?'

She got to her feet in one swift, angry movement. 'Oh, this is impossible. Maybe I'm the one who should move to Midhampton.'

'No.' He rose too. 'No—I apologise. You're right.

We've got to shelve our own problems and unite this last time for him. We both owe him that.'

'Yes.' Joanna bent her head. 'It's been rather a long day. I think I'll go to bed.'

'I'll come up as well, once I've seen to the dogs. Do they still sleep in the rear hall?'

Joanna nodded. She'd pleaded tiredness, but she knew she would not sleep. Her stomach was in knots and her pulse-rate was going haywire.

She took the coffee tray back to the kitchen and then went upstairs. Gabriel caught up with her as she reached the gallery.

'Where have you put me?' His mouth curled slightly. 'Not in your room, I'm sure.'

'That's hardly likely.' She felt defensive colour invade her face.

But Gabriel wasn't looking at her. He'd turned to stare down the length of the gallery to the door which led to the master suite. His voice sounded abrupt—almost remote. 'And not in there, I hope.'

'No,' she said quickly. 'I thought for the time being—your old room.'

He was very still, his gaze fixed on the closed door as if nothing else existed in that moment. His face was haggard, suddenly, and the tawny eyes were filled with a pain too deep for words.

The leopard, Joanna thought suddenly, was wounded. No longer the cool, invulnerable conqueror, but someone she wasn't sure she recognised any more.

She felt her own hurt, her own grief well up inside her in response. Her hand went out to touch his arm. Her lips parted to say his name.

Then a door halfway down the gallery opened and Cynthia came out. She was wearing a white satin dressing gown, and her hair was loose on her shoulders. She had no make-up on and her eyes were red, as if she'd been crying non-stop for hours.

She looked, Joanna thought, about twenty years old.

Cynthia stared at Gabriel, her mouth trembling. 'I thought I heard your voice,' she said huskily. 'Thank God you've come. It's been so awful.' Her voice broke. 'So terrible. Oh, Gabriel, darling.'

She ran to him, burying her face in his shoulder, her whole body shaking as she pressed against him. And his arms closed round her, holding her.

It was, Joanna thought dispassionately, a brilliant performance. But somehow she had no desire to see any more of it.

She turned and went into her own room, shutting the door behind her, wishing, as she did so, that she could shut out the image of Gabriel and Cynthia together with equal ease.

And knowing, with heart-chilling certainty, that it was impossible.

CHAPTER FOUR

IT WILL all be over soon. Joanna, smiling, shaking hands with departing mourners, heard the words echoing in her head over and over again like a mantra.

It was her own personal act of faith, she thought defiantly. Something to cling to in the ongoing nightmare of the past few days.

It had almost been a relief to lose herself in the beauty of the funeral service that morning. The ancient parish church had been crowded, the affection and emotion from the congregation almost tangible.

She had walked composedly up the aisle with Gabriel at her side, and if significant glances and whispered comments had been exchanged she hadn't noticed them.

The only distraction from the age-old words of sorrow and farewell had been Cynthia's ostentatiously muffled sobbing. But then her behaviour had been over the top all week, Joanna thought wearily.

Her stepmother, constituting herself chief mourner, had plagued the staff with constant demands for service. She'd also criticised all the arrangements for the funeral, from the choice of hymns to the food being served at the buffet, but without offering any alternatives or assistance.

And she had barely let Gabriel out of her sight.

Not that he seemed to object, Joanna admitted fairly, although he'd never appeared to pay her a great deal of attention in the past.

But she wouldn't have welcomed it then, either,

because she'd been engaged in her single-minded pursuit of Lionel.

Cynthia had even persuaded Gabriel to drive her to London, with the plea that she had nothing suitable to wear at the funeral. No doubt she had also coaxed him to foot the bill for the mountain of elegant carrier bags and boxes she'd brought back with her.

Watching her descend the stairs that morning, dressed from head to foot in black and wearing a hat with a veil, Joanna had hoped he would feel his money had been well spent.

Perhaps he thought that Joanna herself should have made more of an effort, she'd speculated, hugging the comfort of her navy wool coat around her.

Back at the house, Cynthia had stationed herself on one of the sofas in the drawing room, looking ethereal and accepting condolences as if she were Lionel's widow.

Or Gabriel's future wife.

The thought stabbed at Joanna like a knife in the ribs. But she could no longer doubt the seriousness of Cynthia's purpose. Not having seen her in action over the past few days.

It doesn't matter, she told herself steadily. It can't matter, because when it happens I'll be long gone and far away.

In the meantime she had to cope as best she could, accepting the sympathy and good wishes of their friends and neighbours.

'You're looking very pale, my dear,' said the wife of the local MP. 'I've told that charming husband of yours that he should take you away for some winter sun. A second honeymoon, perhaps,' she added archly.

Joanna, encountering a sardonic look from Gabriel

standing only a few feet away, coloured to the roots of her hair and muttered something disjointed.

People were beginning to drift away, and while Gabriel was outside on the drive saying a few last goodbyes Joanna took the opportunity to go up to her room.

One more ordeal—the reading of the will—to be faced, and then she could get on with her life, she thought, picking up a comb and running it through her hair.

Mrs MP, however out of touch with a particular local situation she might be, had nevertheless been right about one thing.

Joanna did indeed look pale. And subdued, and drab and totally unexciting in her cream lambswool polo-neck sweater and pleated navy skirt, she added silently, pulling a face at her reflection. Although her uninteresting appearance was probably no bad thing, under the circumstances.

She didn't want to be noticed, she reminded herself. She wanted to fade into the background and then disappear altogether and without trace.

Now she lingered at the window, reluctant to return downstairs, even though she knew Henry Fortescue would have been buttonholed by Cynthia by now, and be looking for rescue.

It had snowed overnight, and a faint powdering still touched the top fields with white. The sky was unremittingly grey, and the whole landscape looked bleak and frozen.

Like me, she thought ironically. But the weather suits the day. Brilliant sunshine wouldn't have been appropriate at all.

With a sigh, she turned away from the starkness of winter and surveyed her room instead.

She'd started to pack up some of her more service-able things, sorting them from the smart clothes and cocktail wear, which could go to the local charity shop, and putting them in the old suitcase which she'd arrived with all those years ago. Not in the matched luggage which had accompanied her on honeymoon, she thought, swallowing. That would stay behind with her jewellery, already collected together in its leather case. Only her wedding ring remained, but that was purely temporary.

And she'd been through the classified ads in the county newspaper, looking for possible posts as resident housekeeper, and had written to several of the most likely. If all went well, she could be gone within the week.

But she would miss this room, and the refuge it had provided for so long. Not least in the past two years.

She would probably miss the Manor itself, although it had already begun to change. With Lionel there had always been noise—raised jovial voices, laughter, dogs barking.

Now the place hummed with a quieter, different kind of energy, as if a powerful dynamo had been switched on. There was a new vibrancy—an edge in the atmosphere.

Lionel's study was now unrecognisable. The day after Gabriel's return, a large van had brought a computer and every electronic aid to communication known to the mind of man. The old desk had been sidelined, and in its place was a vast modern affair, bristling with equipment and reminiscent of Mission Control, Houston.

Clearly Gabriel planned to use the Manor as an extension of his office.

So, he won't be using pressure of work as an excuse to stay away in future, Joanna thought. Perhaps the freedom to do exactly what he wants when he wants isn't quite so important to him any more.

He had taken total control of the house—and only once had she seen that control slip. She had been on her way to bed the previous night when she'd noticed a light in Lionel's room. She'd walked down the passage and through the open door, had seen Gabriel on his knees beside his father's bed, his head buried in his folded arms, his whole body shaking...

For a moment every instinct she possessed had urged her to go to him and comfort him. To pillow his head against her and let him weep out his grief in her arms.

But of course she had done no such thing, just tiptoed away, choking back her own tears. Because it changed nothing.

She looked down at her wedding ring, twisting it nervously on her finger. Really, she should remove it now. The conventions had been observed and she had no further reason to go on wearing it.

She was trying to tug it over her knuckle when there was a brief tap on the door and Gabriel walked in.

There was no way he could have seen what she was doing, but all the same Joanna found herself flushing as she put both hands defensively behind her back.

She lifted her chin. 'I didn't tell you to come in.'

'So what else is new?' he asked with cool derision. He saw the half-packed case, and his brows rose. 'Forward planning, darling?'

'I have to think about my future,' she returned, keeping her tone even.

'Now that my father's safety net has been removed?' He gave her a meditative look. 'You'll find it's a cold, hard world out there, Joanna.'

'Living here,' she said, 'hasn't always been a barrel of laughs.'

'I'm sorry. I'll try and be more amusing from now on.'

She shook her head. 'No need. I shan't be here long enough to care.'

'Will you delay your escape long enough to join us in the drawing room? You're keeping everyone waiting.'

'Then do please start without me,' she said with exaggerated politeness. 'It isn't an occasion I relish.'

'This whole week has been a pretty good imitation of hell,' Gabriel said levelly. 'But you're coming down to the drawing room, and you'll listen to Lionel's last will and testament along with everyone else. Because you're still my wife and your place is beside me. At least for the time being.'

'I'm glad you said that.' While they'd been talking she'd managed to work her ring off her finger. She held it out to him. 'I'll return this to you now. I'm sure you can find a good use for it.'

She saw something flare briefly in his eyes, then vanish.

He said silkily, 'I came across Dad's old riding crop yesterday. I could find an even better use for that. Don't push me too hard, Joanna.'

The silence between them, the space that divided them, crackled with sudden tension.

Joanna bit her lip. 'Careful, Gabriel. That famous charm of yours seems to be slipping.'

'I never remember it cutting much ice with you anyway, darling.' The endearment was almost an insult. 'Now, put the ring back on and come downstairs.

Be a brave girl for just a little longer,' he added derisively.

Shaking with anger, she hesitated, then thrust the ring into her skirt pocket and followed him down to the hall.

Outside the drawing room door, she halted. 'There's something I need to ask you.'

'Yes?' He spoke with thinly veiled impatience.

'The letter I left for you. Did you find it?'

He nodded. 'Found it and read it.'

'So—what did you think?'

He shrugged. 'That what it lacked in style it made up for in content.'

She hung onto her temper. 'That was not what I meant, and you know it. I asked you for a quick, no-fault divorce. I'd appreciate an answer.'

'Yes or no? Right here and now?' His brow lifted.

'Please. If it's not too much trouble,' she added icily.

'Not at all.' He was silent for a moment, observing her flushed face, the mutinous tilt of her chin. 'The answer's yes, Joanna. You can have your divorce. And the sooner the better. We'll discuss the details later.'

As her lips parted in shock, he took her arm and propelled her into the drawing room.

She felt suddenly blank, emptied of all emotion. But why should she feel like that? After all, she'd got exactly what she wanted—what she needed. And she should be jubilant. Or as jubilant as the present circumstances allowed, she amended hurriedly.

She saw Cynthia's sidelong glance as they passed, and had to repress a malicious impulse to give her a 'thumbs-up'.

Apart from her stepmother, and Henry Fortescue,

the room was occupied by Mrs Ashby with her husband Tom, who was the head gardener, Graham Welch, the estate manager, Sadie, the groom, and the rest of the staff.

Joanna wanted to shout her freedom aloud, but common sense told her this was neither the time nor the place. For the next half-hour at least she would continue to play her designated role.

But then we'll see, she thought.

Teeth gritted, she allowed herself to be taken to a chair, managing not to flinch as Gabriel perched himself beside her on its arm, his hand resting on her shoulder in apparent solicitude.

Henry Fortescue did not waste time on lengthy explanations. The bulk of Lionel's estate, he said, went to Gabriel, but there were a few personal bequests, and he would begin with the smaller ones.

Every member of staff, right down to Mrs Kemp, who came in to clean, had been remembered with characteristic generosity.

'To Cynthia Elcott,' read Mr Fortescue, 'I bequeath the Victorian oil painting known as *Low Tide*, which she always admired.'

Out of the corner of her eye, Joanna saw her stepmother smile complacently and wait to hear the rest of her good fortune.

But that, apparently, was it. Because Mr Fortescue had moved on. 'And to my beloved daughter-in-law, Joanna Catherine Verne, I leave the detached house in Meadow Lane, Westroe, known as Larkspur Cottage.'

Joanna heard Cynthia's gasp of fury, but her attention was fixed almost painfully on the solicitor, who was telling her that Lionel had also arranged for an annuity of fifty thousand pounds a year to be paid to her.

Tears stung her eyes, and her throat closed. She thought, Thank God. I can sell the cottage and move as far away as I want. I could even live abroad. Darling Lionel. He *did* understand.

But Mr Fortescue hadn't finished yet.

'Both these bequests are conditional on the said Joanna Catherine Verne remaining married to my son Gabriel Verne,' his even voice went on. 'And residing with him at Westroe Manor for a year and a day from the reading of this will.'

The silence which followed was absolute. Joanna could feel all the faces in the room turned towards her, could sense the discreet surprise, Cynthia's narrowed eyes, and, above all, Gabriel's fingers tightening like a vice on her shoulder.

She wanted to cry out—*no*—but her throat refused to utter the sound.

She stared at Mr Fortescue, her eyes pleading with him to say it was all a sick joke. That Lionel couldn't have imposed such a cruel—such an unworkable restriction on her.

But the lawyer's tall figure seemed to be receding, becoming smaller in some strange way, as if she was looking down the wrong end of a telescope.

She tried feebly to wrench away from Gabriel's hold and follow Henry Fortescue—appeal to him— but suddenly there was only darkness, and she fell forward into it.

A voice was saying her name insistently, over and over again. A voice she didn't want to hear, that made her moan feebly in rejection.

She opened unwilling eyes and found herself

stretched out on one of the sofas. Gabriel was sitting on its edge, facing her, holding a glass of water.

'What happened?' She struggled to sit up, looking round the deserted room. 'Where is everybody?'

'I sent them away when you fainted.' His tone was matter-of-fact.

'Fainted?' she echoed. 'But I've never fainted in my life.'

'There's always a first time for everything.' He paused. 'Now, lie still, and drink some of this.' He held the glass to her lips, and Joanna forced herself to swallow.

'Everyone was very understanding,' he went on silkily. 'They all realise what terrible stress you've been under all week.'

Her head was swimming unpleasantly, and she leaned back against the cushions, closing her eyes.

She said wearily, 'They don't know the half of it.'

She felt vaguely nauseous, and made herself drink some more water.

At last she ventured to look at Gabriel. His face was expressionless, the tawny eyes hooded and meditative.

She said, 'I—I'm sorry for behaving so stupidly. It was just such a shock.' She shook her head. 'I still can't believe that Lionel would do something like that to me.'

'You make it sound as if you're the only sufferer.'

There was a note in his voice which alarmed her. She realised suddenly that under that cool, detached exterior, Gabriel was blindingly, blazingly angry.

'But I,' he went on, mockingly, 'chose not to faint.'

Joanna gasped. 'I didn't do it deliberately. That's not fair.'

'Very little is.' His voice bit.

'You don't have to worry,' she said quickly. 'I'll refuse the bequest. I'm allowed to do that.'

'Then you'd be a fool.' His tone was brusque. 'And anyway, there'd be no point.'

'What do you mean?' She stiffened.

'I mean, my dear wife, that I've rethought our marital arrangements. I've decided to obey Lionel's wishes, so our divorce is off.'

Joanna sat up, her startled eyes widening, aware of a pounding in her temples.

'But you can't do that.'

'On the contrary. I can, and just have,' he returned. 'In a year and a day we can think again. But for now we'll just have to make the best of it.'

'There is no "best".' Her voice rose. 'It's an impossible situation.'

'Not if we lay some ground rules in advance.'

'Rules of your making, naturally.' She glared at him.

'I'm prepared to be reasonable,' he said. 'However, I've no intention of fading into obscurity for the next twelve months simply to indulge your sensitivities. My exile is over. This is my home, and I'm going to live in it.'

'Fine,' she said. 'Then you won't object if I move into Larkspur Cottage.'

'I'm afraid I must. The terms of the will stipulate that you live here.'

She bit her lip. 'But we could come to some private arrangement about that, surely.'

'Unfortunately the bequest is already public property. We seem doomed to share a roof—but not for eternity.'

'Think again,' she advised curtly. 'As it happens, I've already made my own plans. I wasn't expecting a legacy on that scale from Lionel, and I don't need it. I mean to earn my own living.'

'Doing precisely what?'

She said, with a touch of defiance, 'I'm applying for a post as a residential housekeeper.'

Gabriel's brows lifted. 'Aren't you a little young for that?' he enquired gently.

'I've been running this house for the past two years,' Joanna reminded him defensively. 'I'm hardly without experience.'

'But you've no references,' he pointed out softly. 'And without them you haven't a prayer of finding a residential job. People have a right to know who's moving in with them.'

Joanna's brows drew together. She said slowly, 'But you, surely, would...'

Her voice trailed away as she saw him shaking his head.

'No way, my dear wife.'

'Don't call me that.' She was trembling again.

'No?' His mouth curled. 'But you are my wife, Joanna, and the next twelve months seem set to cost me very dear, so it seems appropriate.'

She took a deep breath and leaned forward. 'Gabriel—stop playing these games. You don't—you can't want me here. And I don't want to stay. I promise I won't ask you for a thing. So why not just—let me go?'

'Because it isn't what my father wanted. He cared about you, Joanna. He clearly wanted you to have a breathing space. A period of reflection while you make some sensible decisions about what to do with the rest of your life. I'm damned sure he didn't envisage you as a skivvy for some stranger. I intend to respect his wishes. It's that simple.'

'And if I just—go, anyway?' She stared her defiance at him.

'Then you can forget the cosy divorce.' His tawny gaze returned her challenge. 'Because I won't consent. I'll make you wait for every long year the law allows, and even then you'll have a fight on your hands.' He paused. 'So what are you going to do, Joanna?'

She said tautly, 'It would be nice to think I could make a genuine choice. But you seem to have thought of everything.' She looked at him scornfully. 'Tell me, Gabriel, what's it like to always get your own way?'

'If you think this is the way I'd have picked, then your fainting fit must have addled your brain.' He rose to his feet. 'Live here, Joanna, behave yourself, and when the year and a day is up I'll give you your divorce and the most glowing reference you could ask for. Is it a deal?'

'I—guess it has to be.' She swung her feet to the floor and stood, too.

'Graciously spoken, as always,' he murmured. 'What did you do with your wedding ring?'

'It's in my pocket.'

He held out a hand. 'Give it to me.'

Reluctantly, Joanna obeyed. Gabriel stood for a moment, looking at the plain gold circlet as if he had never seen it before.

Then he said abruptly, 'Now your hand.'

Slowly she unclenched a tense fist and extended it towards him. He slid the ring onto her finger.

'I'm sure you've no wish to repeat our vows.' There was a note of mockery and something less easy to analyse in his voice. 'However, I feel I should seal this solemn moment somehow.'

His hands descended on Joanna's shoulders, drawing her inexorably towards him. He said softly, 'So, I'll kiss the bride.'

She wanted to say no—to pull away. But the arms that closed round her were too strong, too determined. And his mouth was too warm, too compelling, stifling the rejection before it could be uttered.

He kissed her slowly and sensuously, as if he had all the time in the world. As if he imagined she would welcome the pressure of his lips parting hers, the silken invasion of his tongue. As if there had been no pain, no disillusionment, and no parting between them.

He held her captive in one arm, allowing his other hand to make a lingering pilgrimage down her spine, from the fragile nape of her neck to the curve of her hip.

Joanna felt her whole body shiver in a response she was unable to control.

When he lifted his head, he was smiling.

He said lightly, 'If I didn't know better, Jo, I'd swear you almost enjoyed that.'

The knowledge that he could be right did nothing to appease her.

She said thickly, 'Is this part of the ground rules—that you're allowed to—maul me whenever you feel like it?'

'No,' he said. 'Treat it as a momentary lapse—not to be repeated. But don't expect me to apologise.'

He ran a finger down the curve of her flushed cheek, and laughed softly.

'And don't look so stricken, darling. Day One is nearly over. Which leaves only three hundred and sixty-five to go. And they'll soon pass, I promise you.'

He went past her and out of the room, closing the door behind him.

Joanna stood very still, staring blindly in front of her.

She said once again, softly, 'It will all be over soon.'

But this time her mantra gave her no comfort at all.

CHAPTER FIVE

JOANNA decided it would be prudent to spend the rest of the day in her room. She took the latest batch of condolence letters with her, and set about answering them. It wasn't a pleasant task, but it helped divert her mind from the even more disturbing thoughts which threatened to take control.

She was expecting a recriminatory visit from Cynthia, who was bound to be equally displeased at the terms of Lionel's will. But for once her stepmother seemed to be keeping her distance.

Or at least from me, Joanna amended wryly.

When Mrs Ashby tapped on the door to ask about dinner, she simply requested a bowl of soup on a tray.

'And then I'm going to have an early night,' she added quietly. 'So I'd rather not be disturbed.'

'Very good, madam.' Mrs Ashby looked down at the carpet. 'Although I understand that Mr Verne and Mrs Elcott are dining at the Crown Hotel this evening.'

Which naturally explained a great deal, Joanna thought when she was alone again.

She changed into nightdress and robe, and drank her soup in the chair by the small but cheerful fire— a bedroom comfort to which Lionel had been strongly addicted, she recalled sadly.

'Radiators aren't cosy,' he'd declare.

She listened to the radio for a while, then got into bed and tried to read, but the words of the book danced meaninglessly in front of her eyes. She tried to sleep, but her mind was running in restless circles and would not let her relax. Her body moved uneasily under the covers, seeking a comfort she could not find.

Now there were no more barricades to shelter her from the fact that Gabriel's kiss had totally unnerved her. And just as disturbing was the realisation that she hadn't resisted him. She hadn't even slapped his face afterwards. And she should have done.

She should have shown him once and for all that his behaviour was unacceptable and would not be tolerated.

The warm, familiar taste of his mouth haunted her. Made her shiver again in what was, she told herself defensively, revulsion.

He had no right, she thought feverishly, and repeatedly. I gave him no right.

But then Gabriel had never waited to be granted favours of any kind, least of all sexual. He had always taken what he wanted, right from the first.

He'd forced her to accept his kiss with the same ruthlessness with which he'd imposed the terms of the will upon her.

Tomorrow she would find out about the divorce laws, she told herself broodingly. See if there was any way round the situation that Gabriel hadn't thought of.

Some hopes, she mocked herself savagely.

She couldn't really believe that he would contest the legal break-up of their marriage, or make her wait the eternity he'd threatened. He was simply using the possibility as a weapon to make her do what he wanted. But why?

She shook her head, staring into the darkness. He

must want to put an end to this sterile situation as much as she did.

Pride seemed the only answer. Gabriel would not want it known that his wife was willing to sacrifice Lionel's generosity in order to be free of him.

Well, he might have prepared the corner, and forced her into it, but from now on she would state her own terms for enduring this—farce.

At last she found herself drifting in and out of an uneasy sleep, hearing the long-case clock in the gallery chime every hour. And realising that she had not heard Gabriel and Cynthia return.

It was almost a relief when Mrs Ashby arrived punctually with her morning tea and she didn't have to pretend any more that she was resting.

The housekeeper gave her a concerned look. 'Are you going to stay in bed today, madam? Shall I call the doctor?'

'No, and no.' Joanna forced a reassuring smile. 'I have a lot of things to see to.'

'Yes, Mrs Verne.' The other woman hesitated awkwardly. 'Will you want me to move your things—to the master bedroom? Mr Gabriel told me last night he wanted it to be prepared, and I didn't know…'

Joanna's smile felt as if it had been welded there.

'Mr Gabriel's arrangements are his own business, Mrs Ashby. However, while I remain at the Manor I shall continue to use this room.'

'Yes, of course, madam.' The older woman's kind face was a picture of embarrassment. 'What about all the late Mr Verne's things?'

Joanna bit her lip. 'I'll speak to Mr Gabriel. Ask what he wants done. Then we'll sort through them together.'

That was one difficult moment survived, she

thought resignedly when she was alone again, but there would undoubtedly be more to follow.

She followed her usual routine of pouring her tea, then taking the cup into the bathroom while she ran a bath for herself, scenting it generously with foaming bath oil in a clove carnation fragrance.

By the time she'd finished her tea, the water was just as she liked it. She slipped off her chiffon nightdress and slid with a sigh into the perfumed bubbles, closing her eyes and leaning back against the quilted headrest.

Usually she had her day mapped out, but now, in spite of her positive words to Mrs Ashby, she had no clear idea of what lay ahead of her.

Did Gabriel wish her to go on running the house in the old way, or did he plan to give the orders now?

That was something else she would have to ask him about, she reflected without pleasure. She tried to think of a way to frame the question that wouldn't sound as if she was pleading for her old status.

'It's dangerous to sleep in the bath. Or is this a planned drowning?'

Because she'd been thinking about him, it took Joanna a couple of seconds to realise that Gabriel's faintly amused drawl was not just in her mind.

She gasped, nearly inhaling a mouthful of bubbles, her head turning in shock towards the bathroom door.

He was lounging in the doorway, totally at ease, the tawny eyes scanning the concealing foam with lazy appreciation.

'What the hell are you doing here?'

Joanna remembered just in time not to sit up.

'I came to tell you I'm going to be away for some while,' he returned. 'I have a meeting in Paris, and another in Vienna later in the week.'

'All right, you've told me,' she said tersely. 'Now you can get out.'

Gabriel's brows lifted. 'I can't say your manners have improved during our separation,' he remarked coldly. 'Not that it makes any real difference. I'll leave when I'm ready.'

'In other words, I'm to be allowed no privacy at all,' Joanna said with a snap.

'If that was really the case,' he said gently, 'you wouldn't have been alone in that bed last night. And you'd certainly have my company in that bath this morning.' He watched a wave of indignant colour invade her face and nodded. 'So stop being absurd and listen.'

She said between her teeth, 'Yes, master.'

He laughed. 'You're getting the idea. Did Mrs Ashby speak to you about Lionel's room?'

'She mentioned it.' Joanna hesitated, the image of him kneeling beside Lionel's bed in her mind. 'Isn't this a—little soon?'

'Perhaps,' he said. 'But I don't want it to turn into some kind of shrine, dusted once a week and everything the way he left it. I want life to get back to normal round here as soon as possible.'

'You have a strange idea of normal.' Joanna could feel the water getting colder. She was also becoming cramped through lying so still, but she dared not move.

'Why, darling,' he said mockingly, 'is this your shy way of telling me you'd like ours to be a conventional marriage?' He shrugged off his jacket, tossed it onto a chair, and began to loosen his tie. 'Perhaps I'll join you after all.'

'You'll do nothing of the kind.' The breath caught in her throat as Gabriel moved across to the bath and

sat down on its broad rim. 'Go away.' Her voice
sounded hoarse and uneven. 'Get out of here. Now.'

He said, 'No, darling. Not quite yet.'

Paralysed, Joanna watched his hand descend towards the surface of the water. For a moment Gabriel
allowed it to hover tantalisingly, barely an inch from
her quivering body, then he scooped up some of the
fragrant foam, lifting it to his face.

He said softly, 'Now this evokes some memories.
Each time I've encountered clove carnations in the
past two years, I've thought of the scent of your skin
in the darkness.'

'Don't expect me to be flattered,' Joanna returned
grittily.

'No, I accept that's too much to hope for.' His dark
face inscrutable, he gently blew the bubbles from his
palm. 'Don't you have any memories, Joanna?'

'None that I care to recall.' Her tone was curt.

'And no curiosity, either? Haven't you ever wondered how it might be between a man and a woman?
Or how it should be?'

'Never.'

'That's a shame.' Gabriel dipped an idle hand into
the water again. Joanna remained like a statue, determined not to flinch. 'Because I've wondered a great
deal—about you, about myself. About the fact that
we're both two years older, and, hopefully, wiser.
That maybe there are things we could both learn from
each other—before we part.'

His smile slanted down at her, and she felt deep
inside her an answering twist of pain, mixed with—
what? Regret—yearning? She couldn't be sure. And
didn't want to find out.

'I mean,' he went on softly, moving the water
gently with his fingers, 'I wouldn't want you to go

out into the world thinking those few doomed en-
counters between us was all there was to it.'

'So what are you offering?' Joanna loaded her tone
with contempt. 'A quick course in sexual gratifica-
tion?' She shook her head. 'Not for me. But I'm sure
you won't lack for willing applicants,' she added cut-
tingly. 'You never have.'

'What a pity.' The tawny gaze undertook another
lingering survey. 'Because those pretty bubbles are
beginning to melt, opening up all kinds of interesting
perspectives. Sure you won't change your mind?'

'Certain.' She was trembling inside, but somehow
managed to keep her tone even. 'And now may I
make something clear?' She drew a deep breath. 'If
this kind of—harassment continues, it's going to
make it impossible for me to remain here—whatever
the consequences.'

'Sexual harassment between husband and wife?'
His brows drew together meditatively. 'I wonder if
that exists in law?'

'I neither know nor care,' she returned steadily.
'I'm not talking legalities, but on a personal level.
You may find these—games of yours amusing, but I
don't. The only way this arrangement can work is by
each of us keeping out of the other's way.'

'You really think that's the sole solution?'

'I know it is.'

He shrugged. 'Then we'll play it your way. God
forbid my foul lust should drive you away,' he added
derisively. He bent forward, running a hand swiftly
over her bare shoulder. 'And you're freezing. It's time
you came out of that water.' He got up and fetched
the towelling robe which hung on the bathroom door.
'Here, put this on,' he directed brusquely.

Freezing? Suddenly she was burning, consumed by some strange and terrifying flame.

She set her teeth. 'In my own good time.'

He laughed. 'You mean you'd rather risk pneumonia than allow me a fleeting glimpse of you naked? Now, are you underestimating my self-control—or overestimating the effect of your own charms? However, we won't debate the point now.'

'Or ever,' she snapped back.

'All avenues of communication safely closed off?' He shook his head. 'You disappoint me, sweetheart. But from now on it'll be strictly business.'

He draped the robe unhurriedly within reach, directed one last appreciative look downwards, then became instantly and impersonally brisk, leaving Joanna to grind her teeth in impotent rage.

'With regard to Lionel's clothes and belongings. I'd like them stored in another room, please, so I can go through them at my leisure.'

'If that's what you want,' she acknowledged stiffly.

'It isn't, particularly.' Gabriel grimaced. 'It's a lousy job, but I can't, in conscience, wish it on anyone else.'

He picked up his jacket, slung it over one shoulder, and turned to go. Then he paused. 'By the way, one last thought.' His tone was abrupt, and Joanna tensed again. 'As Larkspur Cottage is empty, why don't you rent it to Cynthia for the next twelve months? Apparently she's always had a hankering to live there.'

'I suppose you discussed it last night—over the *hors d'oeuvres*?' Joanna made her tone poisonously sweet, then regretted it.

But he smiled at her, unfazed. 'Over the coffee and Armagnac, actually. But it's entirely up to you. It's going to be your property, after all. Think it over, and tell her your decision.'

Then he was gone. And a moment later she heard her bedroom door close.

She sat up gingerly, feeling slightly giddy. As she glanced down she realised with annoyance that her nipples had tautened to hard, rosy peaks in the cooling water, and hoped very much that they weren't one of the perspectives Gabriel had referred to.

She climbed out, reaching for the robe and huddling it on with a shiver, thankful that it wasn't Gabriel's hands arranging the folds of fabric around her.

As it might have been. And the shock of that realisation made her breathless. As, indeed, had her body's helpless reaction to the brief touch of his hand on her shoulder.

If this unwanted confrontation had taught her anything, it was that she was by no means impervious to Gabriel, and she needed to be.

She would have to armour herself somehow, she thought grimly. And his absence over the next few days would give her the opportunity to do so.

Nor would she again allow herself to be this physically vulnerable. She would call a locksmith immediately, and have her bedroom door made secure.

But how to keep the thought of him out of her heart—and the remembrance of him out of her bloodstream—was another matter entirely.

She would give Sadie a hand in the stables, Joanna decided as she dressed in breeches, boots and a heavy sweater, and then she'd help her exercise her charges. Some strenuous hard work was what she needed to take her mind off her personal problems. Besides, the horses hadn't had much attention in the past few days, and would probably be kicking down the doors of their boxes.

She wondered what Gabriel would do with Nutkin, the gelding Lionel had been riding when he died. He was a strong, powerful beast, and Joanna wasn't altogether sure she could handle him, or if she even ought to try.

She sighed silently as she descended the stairs. This was just one of the matters needed a decision from Gabriel. She would have to make a list.

As she reached the foot of the stairs she encountered Cynthia, just emerging from the dining room. Joanna, aware that her stepmother rarely stirred out of her room until midday, gave her a surprised look.

'Could I have a word?' Cynthia's expression was that of a cat who'd been awarded if not the cream, a very large saucer of milk.

'Fine.' Joanna paused. 'Is there any coffee left?'

'Plenty. Why?'

Joanna shrugged. 'We may as well make any discussion as civilised as possible,' she countered, walking into the dining room and filling a cup from the heavy silver pot.

'Darling.' Cynthia draped herself decoratively on one of the high-backed dining chairs. 'I'm perfectly prepared to be as civilised as you could wish.'

Provided you do as I want, Joanna supplied silently.

She took the chair opposite. 'I suppose this concerns Larkspur Cottage.'

'It does indeed.' Her stepmother assumed a vaguely injured expression. 'I can't imagine what Lionel was thinking of to leave the place to you. I thought that he and I were in complete agreement about it.'

Joanna bit her lip. 'I don't think Lionel was considering anyone's personal wishes when he drew up his will.'

'No.' Cynthia's eyes sparked with sudden malice. 'Or he wouldn't have put in that absurd clause about Gabriel having to stay married to you for another year. The poor sweet looked positively murderous when it was read out.'

'Indeed,' Joanna said politely. 'Then what a pity I only fainted instead of actually dropping dead from shock. Think of the trouble it would have saved.'

Cynthia's crimson lips tightened. 'What nonsense you talk sometimes.'

'Well, you won't have to put up with it much longer,' Joanna said cheerfully. 'Not if you move to Larkspur Cottage.'

'Then you're willing to rent it to me?' Cynthia sounded surprised.

'Why not?'

Her stepmother shrugged. 'It occurred to me that you might try to put a spoke in my wheel. Play dog in the manger.' A slight acid entered her voice.

'If it comes to that, the place doesn't actually belong to me yet,' Joanna pointed out levelly. 'Henry Fortescue and Gabriel are joint executors. Presumably they have no objection.'

'Well, Gabriel certainly doesn't.' Cynthia stretched voluptuously. 'It was all his own idea.' She looked at Joanna from under her lashes. 'But I don't suppose he told you that. After all, it wouldn't be very tactful—under the circumstances.'

Joanna had the strangest feeling that she'd just been pierced to the heart with a spear of ice.

Her voice, too, seemed to be coming from some far distance. And to belong to a stranger. 'In other words, it's more convenient for both of you to conduct your affair under a different roof. No, he'd hardly be likely to mention that.'

Cynthia shrugged again. 'Naturally, he'd want to spare your feelings, darling. While you're still officially his wife, that is.'

Joanna recovered herself. 'But you, clearly, have no such compunction.' Her tone was dry.

Cynthia laughed. 'Well, I'd already told you my intentions.'

'Does Gabriel know that?'

'Well, hardly.' Cynthia's tone was dismissive. 'Men are such egotists, darling. He wouldn't want to know you'd given your permission, as it were. I expect, in his heart of hearts, he'd much prefer to think you minded—that you still cared—a little.'

She got to her feet. 'Now I think I'll go and have a look round the cottage. It's partly furnished, I know, but there are things I'll need to get.' She smiled slowly. 'A bigger bed, for starters.' She paused, allowing that to be absorbed. Then, 'Tell Mrs Ashby that I won't be in for lunch, there's a dear.'

Joanna watched her leave the room. Her whole body ached with tension, and there was a weird drumming in her ears.

Cynthia's news should have come as a welcome relief, yet its effect had been the opposite. She felt dizzy—crucified with emotional pain. And she knew why, and for the first time was prepared to admit it.

'I do mind.' She said the anguished words aloud. 'God help me, I do care. And somehow I'm going to have to live with this.'

She shook her head. How could she have been such a fool—so blind, so stubborn? How had she failed to see that even the fiasco of their failed marriage could not kill the love and longing that Gabriel had always engendered in her? Pride and a sense of betrayal might have driven it underground, but could never destroy it.

And this was the truth she now had to face. Now, at the very moment that Gabriel had chosen to begin an affair.

Somehow, she told herself, I've got to hide the pain and simply pretend—to Cynthia, to the staff, to all our friends and acquaintances. And to Gabriel. She swallowed. Oh, God, particularly to Gabriel. I must never—ever let him know. I've told him the marriage is over—if it ever really began—and that's how it must remain.

She drew a deep breath. He's creating a new life for himself. And whatever I may think about it, it's what he's chosen, she thought, biting her lip until she could taste blood. And I've got to do the same. Because hoping that Gabriel might change—that he might love me as his wife in the way that I need to be loved—is a futile exercise.

Oh, he'd take me to bed, if I gave him the chance. He's no angel, after all, and I must be one of his few failures, so he has something to prove. But it wouldn't change a thing—because sex without love is meaningless—a travesty, and I couldn't bear it.

So, by holding him at arm's length I've done something right, at least, even if I didn't realise it at the time.

She lifted her chin. She'd made believe that she didn't love Gabriel—didn't want him—for nearly three years. Up to a few minutes ago she'd even deceived herself. Until another woman—and Cynthia, of all people—had shown her the truth about herself.

She thought, If I can go on pretending for another year.

But she knew, all the same, in spite of her brave thoughts, that ahead of her were the twelve longest, loneliest and most desolate months of her entire life.

CHAPTER SIX

WORK kept her going, coupled with the kindness of friends and neighbours. She rode out each day with Sadie, took the dogs for long walks, helped clear the winter debris from the garden, and worked out a regime for spring cleaning the entire house with Mrs Ashby.

They began, as instructed, with the massive master bedroom, packing Lionel's clothes and personal effects into boxes in a strained and careful silence. The room had been decorated the previous year, so all that was really needed, after a thorough cleaning, was to change the curtains at the windows and around the massive four-poster bed.

Lionel had favoured a rather florid deep red, but Joanna found some much lighter drapes in a subtle olive-green, and these were pressed and hung.

For the bed she chose the best Irish linen sheets and pillowcases, adding a quilted satin coverlet that combined the olive of the curtains with shades of amber and dark brown in an intricate pattern. But she couldn't bring herself to assist Mrs Ashby in making it up. There was only so much she could reasonably be expected to stand, she thought, beating a hasty retreat on the mendacious grounds that Sadie needed her in the stables.

Not that Gabriel would be spending many nights there anyway.

She found she was spending as much time away from the house as she could, accepting with genuine gratitude the invitations to lunch and dinner that were pressed on her by local people.

Some of the invitations, she knew, were impelled by curiosity too. Rumours of Lionel's will and its strange provisions had inevitably leaked out, and people, aware of the separation between Gabriel and herself, were bound to speculate—and attempt a little delicate probing.

Joanna stone-walled the questions, and evaded committing herself about the future.

Not difficult, when she herself had no idea where she would go or what she would do.

On the face of it, she could take the easy option. Endure the year, then find a property well away from Westroe and its memories, and live on the income that Lionel had provided for that purpose. But she knew that wouldn't do.

I've hidden from life for too long already, she thought. I need a career—some direction to my existence. Something that will stop me thinking...

But none of the plans she hatched for herself during the restless nights held any appeal in the merciless light of morning.

Get through one day at a time, she adjured herself. That's as much as you can hope for at present.

Cynthia's coming removal to Larkspur Cottage had also aroused discreet comment, but again Joanna refused to be drawn.

Anyway, if the local grapevine was working with its usual efficiency, they would all soon know what the score was, she thought unhappily. And then she'd have to endure them all feeling sorry for her.

Their sympathy for her over Lionel she could welcome, but to be pitied because her husband was having a blatant fling with her stepmother was a very different matter.

Cynthia's preparations were in full swing already. She was rarely at the Manor during the day at all, which, as Joanna silently admitted, suited her fine.

Henry Fortescue was drawing up a lease for the cottage, although he'd looked down his nose at the token rent which Joanna had suggested. But then he probably didn't realise who would actually be paying it, Joanna reminded herself. And it was not her business to tell him.

'How does Mrs Elcott intend to earn her living?' Henry Fortescue had looked sternly over his glasses. 'You've been extremely generous over the rent, but she will still have the local tax to pay, and heating bills.' He paused. 'The allowance which Lionel paid her as your companion ceased on his death, of course.'

Joanna looked at the floor. 'I believe Gabriel intends to continue it.' She kept her face and voice expressionless.

'Quite extraordinary,' Mr Fortescue said dourly.

Not when you knew the facts, Joanna thought unhappily, although Gabriel must be totally besotted to let her manipulate him like this.

He'd telephoned each evening while he was away, and Cynthia had taken the calls. Try as she would, Joanna could not avoid the sound of her voice, speaking softly and intimately, with the occasional husky giggle, although thankfully she could not make out exactly what was being said.

It would be a relief, she thought, when Cynthia actually moved herself to the cottage and she no longer had to see or hear what was going on. And if she could have her imagination removed by some kind of lobotomy, that would be a bonus too.

'By the way, darling,' Cynthia said casually over breakfast, a few days before Gabriel's projected return. 'You don't mind if I take some things with me to Larkspur?'

'What did you have in mind?' Joanna was going through the post, dividing bills and official communications from personal letters.

Cynthia waved an airy hand. 'Oh, just home comforts. The picture Lionel left me, of course, and a few of the bits and pieces from my room.'

'I presume you've already cleared it with Gabriel.' Joanna slit open an envelope with precision. 'So why ask me?'

'Well, you are the mistress of the house.' Cynthia paused. 'Nominally at least.'

'So I am,' Joanna agreed drily. 'How could I forget?' She looked down at the letter in her hand. 'Oh, the Osbornes are back from Portugal. I'd better go over there this afternoon and see Sylvia. She's obviously terribly upset that they weren't here when it happened.' She picked up the pile of correspondence. 'Do you want to come with me?'

Cynthia studied her nail varnish. 'Absolutely not. Sylvia Osborne's the dullest woman in the neighbourhood, and I can't stand any more weeping and wailing.'

'She's also Gabriel's godmother, and he's very fond of her,' Joanna reminded her levelly. 'And you can hardly call a highly successful landscape painter dull.'

Cynthia shrugged. 'Well, you rush round and admire her latest daub. I've got better things to do.'

'The hairdresser?' Joanna suggested lightly on her way to the door.

'Beauty parlour, actually. A whole day's pampering from my head down to my toes.' Cynthia gave her a cat-like smile. 'I want to be looking and feeling my best when Gabriel returns.' Her smile widened. 'Of course, you don't have to worry about things like that. You do your bit by keeping the dogs and horses happy.'

'I know my place,' Joanna agreed equably, and went out of the room, followed by the dogs. She phoned Sylvia Osborne and left a message on the answering machine, suggesting that she would call over during the afternoon. Then she went out to the stables.

Sadie emerged from the tack room. 'Morning, Jo. Shall I saddle up Minnie for you?'

'Change of plan today.' Joanna gave the elderly mare, who was her usual mount, a consoling pat, and moved on to Nutkin's box. She ran her hand down his handsome nose. 'I'd better give this lad some exercise today. Heaven knows, he needs it.'

Sadie hesitated. 'Mr Gabriel said no one was to ride him but himself,' she offered uncertainly.

'Nonsense,' Joanna said briskly, relegating her own doubts about handling the chestnut to the back of her mind. 'Nutkin can't stand around waiting for him to get back from his European tour. Let's get him tacked up.'

Sadie still held back. 'Mr Gabriel was quite definite about it, Jo. He's not sure about Nutkin's temperament.' Her eyes brimmed suddenly. 'Poor Mr Lionel. I know it wasn't the horse's fault...'

'No,' Joanna said briskly. 'It certainly wasn't, and I won't allow him to be demonised because of it. Don't look so worried, Sadie,' she added more gently.

'Mr Gabriel isn't here, and, anyway, I'll take full responsibility. I'm just going to hack him quietly round the lanes.'

Sadie looked as if this was little consolation, but together they saddled Nutkin, who was inclined to take exception to their attentions.

As Joanna had expected, he was lively in the extreme, and not easy to hold, but he didn't drop his head, or buck to try and unseat her as she eased him, sidling and dancing, out of the yard, the dogs following behind.

'It's all right, my beauty,' she told him softly. 'You and I are going to be friends.'

It wasn't the most comfortable ride she'd ever had. Nutkin was suspicious of everything, and an approaching cyclist had him rooted to the spot, eyes rolling.

Joanna spoke gently and reassuringly, but kept firm control as she urged him past this apparently alarming hazard.

After that it became much easier. The lanes were quiet on a chill, grey morning, and the rest of the ride passed without incident. Until Joanna turned for home.

She noticed something large and white in the hedge ahead of them, and by the way Nutkin began to fidget and toss his head he'd seen it too. As she got closer she realised it was a sheet of newspaper. As they drew level, with Nutkin snorting in protest, the wind caught it and it suddenly ballooned upwards.

Nutkin whinnied in fright and reared upwards, with Joanna clinging onto him for grim death as he plunged and skittered, his hooves sliding on the frosty road.

She heard a shout, and saw a young man—a stranger—running towards her.

'Are you all right?'

'Getting there,' Joanna returned breathlessly.

He grabbed the bridle, and, between them, Nutkin came back under control.

Once Nutkin was quiet, the newcomer walked over to the hedge, seized the offending newspaper and crushed it into a ball which he thrust into the pocket of his quilted jacket.

He came back to Joanna's side and looked up at her. He was tall, with fair hair, and blue eyes which crinkled at the corners when he smiled. He said, 'Thank God you're all right. I really thought you were coming off there. You could have been hurt really badly.'

'But I didn't, and I wasn't.' Joanna was more shaken than she cared to admit, but she returned his smile with an effort. 'But from now I'll ride him up on the hill, where there aren't any stray newspapers or other white flapping things to spook him.' She paused. 'And thank you for your help, too.'

'You didn't really need it. You're one terrific rider.'

She shook her head. 'If I was, I might have seen the problem coming and avoided it.'

It occurred to her that she'd never seen him before, which was unusual out of the holiday season.

She said, 'Are you staying locally?'

'I'm actually living here now. I came down to visit old friends, found they'd moved on, and decided to stay anyway.' He held out his hand. 'I'm Paul Gordon.'

'Verne—Joanna Verne,' Joanna said as they shook hands.

'Is that Miss or Mrs?'

She felt her cheeks warm under the frank appraisal in his blue eyes. 'Mrs,' she returned briefly.

He gave an exaggerated sigh. 'Just my luck. And I was hoping I'd met someone who could show me around—maybe have dinner with me.'

Joanna laughed. 'Sorry about that—but I'm sure you'll soon make friends.'

She heard a rumbling noise and glanced down. Jess and Molly were standing menacingly, legs stiff and hackles raised, as they growled at the newcomer.

'Hey, you two,' Joanna admonished them. 'Everything's fine. Don't be silly.'

'I'm afraid I'm rather nervous of dogs,' Paul Gordon said, grimacing. 'I expect they can sense that.'

'Possibly.' Joanna frowned. 'Yet they're usually very friendly.' She hesitated. 'Well, I'd better be getting back before someone raises an alarm. Thanks again for your help, and—I'll see you around.'

'You can count on it.' He stepped back, lifting a hand in a cheerful salute.

The dogs gave a final throaty bark, and followed her.

'I'm ashamed of you both,' she told them severely. At the corner, she realised she hadn't asked where he was living. She glanced back, but Paul Gordon had disappeared.

As she rode into the stableyard the dogs dashed past her, whimpering joyfully and uttering short, staccato barks of excitement.

With a swift lurch of the heart, she saw Gabriel standing at the door of the tack room waiting for her, his hands thrust into the pockets of his navy overcoat.

Her lips began to curve involuntarily into a smile of welcome, but there was no answering warmth in his expression.

Instinct told her that he was very angry.

She leaned forward, patting the gelding's neck to hide the swift colour which had risen in her face.

Her voice sounded high, and rather brittle. 'Surprise, surprise. You weren't expected back for several days yet.'

'Evidently.' His tone was icy. He looked past her to an apprehensive Sadie, just emerging from one of the loose boxes. 'I gave orders that only I was to ride this horse. Why have I been disobeyed?'

Joanna said quickly, 'It's not Sadie's fault. She told me what you'd said, and I—I overruled her.'

She saw his face darken, and added, 'If you want to talk about it later, then I'll listen. But, for the moment, Nutkin's needs take priority.'

His lips tightened. 'As you wish,' he said with ominous quietness. 'I'll expect you in the study in half an hour.' He turned and walked away towards the house.

As if I were some schoolgirl playing truant, Joanna thought, seething, as she dismounted.

'Oh, Lord,' Sadie said dismally. 'I'd better start looking for another job.'

'Nothing of the kind,' Joanna told her robustly. 'He won't blame you. I'll see to that.'

Without particular haste, and smilingly refusing Sadie's anxious offers of assistance, she rubbed Nutkin down and put his rug on him, then cleaned the tack with her usual care, before hanging it away.

Grace Ashby met her as she entered the house.

'Mr Verne has returned, madam,' she said rather anxiously. 'And he's been asking for you. Several times.'

'Yes, I know,' Joanna returned steadily. 'Bring some coffee to the study, please, Grace.'

The study door was closed. She regarded it for a moment, then tapped lightly and went in.

Gabriel was sitting at the desk, frowningly intent on the computer screen in front of him.

Without looking up, he said, 'I don't appreciate being kept waiting, Joanna.'

She said crisply, 'And I don't like being ordered about as if I were a servant. Or being reprimanded in front of the staff either.'

His head lifted sharply. He gave her a long look. 'Point taken,' he said at last. 'But the difficulty is knowing exactly how to deal with you.

'After all,' he added with deliberation. 'You certainly don't want me to treat you as a wife.' He gave her a barbed smile. 'Or has my absence made your heart grow fonder?'

'No,' she said expressionlessly. 'It has not.'

'The loss,' he said, too courteously, 'is all mine.' He paused. 'However, when I give particular instructions, I expect them to be obeyed—even by you. And I said quite clearly that Nutkin was only to be ridden by me.'

'But you,' she said, 'were on the other side of Europe. Vienna, wasn't it?'

'Vienna was cancelled. My opposite number has appendicitis.'

'Whatever,' she said shortly. 'The point is it's not fair to leave the horse eating his head off in the stables while you charge round the world playing business-man of the year.'

'No,' he said. 'The real point is that you thought I wouldn't find out.' He leaned back in his chair. 'Find him a comfortable ride, did you?'

'He will be,' she said. 'When we're used to each other.'

'Lionel had doubts about him, you know. Wasn't sure he was going to keep him. He thought he spooked too easily.'

She shrugged. 'That can be cured. On the hill there'll be nothing to alarm him.'

'Nor will there be you,' he said. 'At least, not on Nutkin.'

'Lionel never forbade me to ride anything in his stables,' she flashed.

'I don't think he'd have encouraged you to ride Nutkin.'

'Yet here I am, safe and sound.' She put out of her mind the memory of those moments when she'd thought both she and the horse would go down on the road.

'Then let's keep it that way. From now on you ride Minnie or Rupert.'

'Am I supposed to be impressed by this display of autocracy?'

'That's entirely up to you.' He reached for the mail she'd placed on the desk earlier. 'By the way, Sylvia rang back to say this afternoon's fine and ask us to have tea with them. I accepted.'

Joanna stared at him. 'You mean—both of us?'

'Of course. Why not?'

She shook her head. 'I can think of all kinds of reasons. I'll go on my own at a different time.'

He said wearily, 'Joanna—stop being a brat. We shall have to appear in public together from time to time. It's known as satisfying the conventions. Going to Sylvia's will be a painless start.'

That, she thought, is what you think.

Aloud, she said, 'Don't you think your godmother will find it strange to see us playing good companions?'

'On the contrary, she's all for civilised behaviour.' He paused. 'Even if she did think our marriage was a terrible mistake.'

'Yet another one.' Joanna gave a small, metallic laugh. 'The list is endless.'

There was a knock at the door and Grace Ashby came in with a tray of coffee, which Joanna directed her to place on a side table.

When they were alone again, Gabriel's brows lifted mockingly. 'Your idea, darling?' he drawled. 'How very thoughtful of you.'

'Just practising my civilised behaviour.' While the door was open she'd seen Cynthia hovering in the hall, clearly awaiting her chance.

I shouldn't hold up the course of true love any longer, she thought, biting her lip.

'Well,' she continued brightly, 'I'll leave you to it.'

'Stay,' he said. 'Have some coffee with me.'

'Another order?' She looked at him with hauteur.

'Just a simple request.'

'Now, that,' she said, 'I don't believe.'

'Why not?'

'Because simplicity is not one of your primary characteristics.'

'You're wrong,' he said. 'I'm an animal of fairly basic appetites—as I'm sure you remember.' His gaze held hers for what seemed an endless moment. 'But for now my overriding desire is for coffee. Be a good wife and pour me some, will you?'

'Gladly.' She paused. 'Let me see. You take it with cream and two sugars, right?'

'Wrong.' He rocked back gently in his chair. 'Just plain black.'

'Of course,' she said repentantly. 'I must have been thinking of someone else.'

'You wish,' he murmured.

She poured the coffee with exaggerated care and put it beside him, retiring with her own cup to the seat beside the fire.

There was a silence, then Gabriel said abruptly, 'Thank you for sorting out Lionel's room. It can't have been easy.'

'Very little is.'

He gave her an ironic look. Then, 'Did you come to any decision about Larkspur Cottage?'

Her throat muscles tightened. 'I followed up your suggestion, and it's all settled. Cynthia's on the point of moving in.' She hesitated. 'Henry Fortescue seemed concerned about the rent—how it was going to be paid. I—I didn't really know what to tell him.'

'I'll talk to him.' Gabriel made a note on a pad beside him. 'Explain the situation.'

'That—might be best,' Joanna agreed woodenly. She hesitated again. 'Cynthia's suggested taking some of the furnishings from here. Do you wish to make any kind of stipulation about that?'

He shrugged. 'No. Let her take what she wants.'

In other words, give her *carte blanche* to strip the place, Joanna thought bitterly. But why should I care?

She took a deep breath to compose herself. 'Perhaps you'd let me have a schedule of your movements over the next few weeks, so that I can consult Grace about meals,' she suggested with cool politeness.

'That won't be a problem. I shall be remaining here for the foreseeable future.'

Her cup rattled back into its saucer. She said, 'You mean you won't be going abroad again for a while?'

'I shan't be going anywhere.' Gabriel gave her a cordial smile. 'I've delegated the running of the company to my managers, and told them to contact me only in emergency. I have enough on my hands here as executor of the estate at the moment.'

Joanna bit her lip. 'This is—rather a change in policy for you.'

'And probably long overdue.' The tawny eyes rested on her meditatively. 'If I've learned anything from the debacle of our marriage, Joanna, it's been the unwisdom of sacrificing personal relationships to work. I shan't make the same mistake again.'

Somehow, Joanna drank the rest of her coffee, put down her cup, and rose to her feet.

She said quietly, 'I'm sure your future wife will be glad to hear it.'

He smiled faintly. 'I'll make sure she is.' He glanced at his watch. 'Shall we say half past three?'

She stared at him, thrown. 'For what?'

'Our visit to Charles and Sylvia,' he said patiently. 'We'll take my car.'

She wanted to scream at him, Take your future wife instead. But she forced the words back with an effort.

'Actually, I have some errands in Westroe this afternoon,' she improvised swiftly. 'Perhaps it would be better if I met you there.'

'Perhaps.' He rose too, coming round the desk to her. Joanna made herself stand her ground, return his gaze with apparent unconcern.

He said softly, 'Just as long as you don't forget, or find yourself detained by some unforeseen circumstance. Because that, Jo, wouldn't amuse me at all.'

'In other words—your rules.' She kept her tone flat. 'You'll have to supply me with a list of them, Gabriel, in case I inadvertently transgress.'

His eyes glinted at her. 'What—you, my little plaster saint? Impossible.'

'Plaster saint?' she exclaimed, stung. 'That's a foul thing to call anyone.'

'Isn't that what you want to be?' There was no amusement in the tawny gaze now. 'Safe in your little niche—immune from the sins of the flesh—untouchable and—untouched? Because you've never wanted to be a woman, Joanna.' He paused, 'Or was it simply being my woman that was so abhorrent to you?'

His words were like knives, but she made herself shrug lightly.

'Can't we simply agree we were incompatible and leave it there?'

He shook his head slowly. 'You were one of my failures in life, Jo. And I don't like to lose.'

Her heart was hammering against her ribcage. His eyes were like molten gold. She felt them searing her flesh.

She lifted her chin. 'Not a failure, Gabriel. Just—a mistake. From which we can both learn.'

'Or we could choose a different lesson.'

One hand snaked round her, pulling her forward. The other lifted to release her hair from the confines of its prosaic elastic band.

She found herself held against him—imprisoned by his arms.

He said huskily, 'Forget the pious platitudes, Jo. For once in your life kiss me as if you wanted to. As if you wanted me.'

His mouth was so close—just a butterfly's wing away. His hand moved on the nape of her neck, under the fall of her hair, softly, teasingly, sending a deep shiver pulsating through her body.

He whispered, 'Kiss me...'

It would be so easy, she thought longingly, to yield to his persuasion. To let the desire of the moment

sweep her away. To assuage the pain and the need of
the past unhappy years by putting her lips against his.
And by following wherever that led.

Oh, dear God, so disastrously, fatally easy.

She wrenched herself free. Took a step backwards,
distancing herself. Out of harm's way.

She said, between her teeth, 'This is not a game,
Gabriel, and I am not some toy. You don't like to fail.
I won't be used. Checkmate.'

She turned and went out of the room, across the
hall and up the stairs, without looking back and without hesitation, in spite of the scalding tears that were
half blinding her.

Tears that she dared not let him see. Tears she
could not allow herself to shed, because they were a
sign of the weakness she could not afford.

And she knew with painful desperation that she was
going to need all the strength she possessed—just
to survive.

CHAPTER SEVEN

'MY DEAREST child, what a nightmare for you.' Sylvia Osborne's hug was warm, but the look she directed at Joanna was searching as well as kind. 'I can hardly believe it.'

'Nor I.' Joanna's voice was constrained. 'I still look up, expecting him to walk in...'

'Of course.' Sylvia drew her over to one of the comfortable, sagging, chintz-covered sofas and sat down beside her, clasping Joanna's hands in hers. 'If only we'd been here. Not that we could have done anything...' She paused. 'And now Gabriel is back.' She let the words sink into another silence.

Joanna bit her lip. 'Yes. Have you heard the terms of Lionel's will?'

Sylvia nodded. 'Gabriel told me when we spoke on the telephone this morning. It's all quite unbelievable.'

Joanna swallowed. 'He—he's very angry about it, isn't he?'

'Small wonder,' Sylvia said tartly. 'Firstly he's dragooned into that ridiculous marriage—which anyone could see was going to be a disaster, and which one would have thought might have cured Lionel of interfering in other people's lives—and now, in spite of everything, he's being manipulated again.'

'But he doesn't have to be,' Joanna said flatly. 'I've told him I'll renounce my bequest. Go somewhere else. Start a new life. Only he won't allow it.'

'Well, of course not. However muddled his motives, Lionel has provided you with a future. Gabriel wouldn't let you deprive yourself of that.' She shook her head. 'Verne men, my dear. Pride, stubbornness, and a keen sense of honour—particularly where their dependants are concerned.'

'I,' Joanna said very clearly, 'have no wish to be a dependant of Gabriel's.'

'A view he shares, no doubt.' Sylvia paused. 'I thought he was coming with you. What have you done—murdered him and shoved his body out of the car?'

For the first time in many days Joanna heard herself laugh out loud.

'Now why didn't I think of that?' She shook her head. 'He's joining us presently. I—I had some shopping to do, so we decided to arrive here separately.'

As soon as she'd composed herself that morning, Joanna had changed out of her riding gear into skirt and sweater, topped them with her trenchcoat, and driven into Westroe.

She'd lunched on scrambled eggs on toast in a local tea room, and spent the rest of the time mooching grimly round the parade of shops, eventually buying a cream silk shirt that she didn't need simply for appearances.

'Separately, but not that far apart.' Sylvia looked past her through the window. 'Gabriel's here now, surveying the frost damage in the garden with Charles.' She patted Joanna's arm. 'Come and give me a hand with the tea things. In awkward situations, I always find it helps to appear busy.'

No one could feel uptight in Sylvia's kitchen, Joanna thought, arranging sandwiches on plates and filling dishes with jam and cream for the batch of feather-light scones still cooling from the Aga.

Sylvia loved to cook, and she'd created an environment for herself that was warm and homely, as well as being an efficient workspace. Pans and utensils hung from racks, and the huge built-in dresser groaned under the weight of her favourite blue and white china.

'I made a Dundee cake too.' Sylvia passed it to her. 'It's Gabriel's favourite.'

'So it is,' Joanna said slowly. 'I—I'd forgotten.'

'Well, why should you remember?' Sylvia asked robustly. 'It isn't as if you ever cooked for him, after all, and got to know his likes and dislikes. As soon as the honeymoon was over, it was straight back to the Manor and the *status quo*. Not exactly the usual start in marriage that most young wives experience,' she added drily.

Joanna smiled wanly. 'I don't think it made much difference in the long run. As you've already pointed out, it wasn't a marriage made in heaven.'

'But it didn't have to end up in hell, either. Perhaps if you'd had a home of your own—some privacy where you could have slogged out your problems—it might have helped.'

'There was never any question of that.' Joanna arranged cups and saucers carefully on a tray. *Because Gabriel never wanted to be tied down like that. It was convenient for him to leave me at Westroe while he got on with his own life.*

'And there were compensations too,' she said. 'When things were really bad, at least I wasn't alone.'

'No,' Sylvia said with a snap. 'You always had your stepmother, of course. A terrific consolation.' She gave Joanna a steely look. 'I suppose she's sticking to the Manor like glue?'

'Not exactly.' Joanna's hand shook as she poured

milk into a silver jug, causing her to spill some on the worktop. 'She's moving to Larkspur Cottage for the next twelve months or so.' She fetched a cloth and wiped up the milk drops. 'It—it was Gabriel's idea.'

'Ah,' Sylvia said neutrally, 'I see.' She spooned tea into the pot and poured on boiling water. 'So you and Gabriel will be on your own together at last.' She sounded meditative.

'Only to fulfil the terms of the will.' Joanna tipped sugar cubes into a bowl and placed it on the tray. 'And through no wish of mine, believe me.'

'You blame Gabriel for everything, don't you?' Sylvia's voice was wry. 'Would it help if I told you he knew about Lionel's will and did his damnedest to talk him out of it?'

'For his own good reasons, no doubt,' Joanna retorted tightly.

'No, for your sake,' Sylvia returned. 'He wanted you to have your freedom, and without strings. He thought he'd persuaded Lionel to agree.'

For a moment they stood looking at each other, then Joanna turned away.

'I'm sorry,' she said wearily. 'I keep forgetting that he's your godson, and you're bound to be on his side.'

'Nothing of the kind,' Sylvia said briskly. 'I don't condone his past behaviour, and he knows it. He's not a fool, but he's certainly acted like one. I only wish he'd transfer some of his business acumen to his private life.'

She gave a brief sigh, then glanced around her. 'Now, if we're all ready, let's take the tea in.'

Sylvia was right about one thing, Joanna realised. Between the affectionate, exuberant greeting she received from Charles and the handing round of cups and plates of food, Gabriel's cool politeness went almost unnoticed. Almost.

And as the conversation ranged, from the state of the garden to the amount of painting Sylvia had achieved in Portugal, the fact that Joanna and he barely exchanged a word with each other wasn't so painfully evident either.

'Did you know we'd let the Lodge at last?' Charles turned to Gabriel. 'We'd almost begun to give up hope, but the agents found someone while we were away and he's already moved in.'

'Pity we didn't know that Cynthia Elcott was looking for a place.' Sylvia busied herself with the teapot. 'Not that I'd particularly want her for a neighbour, of course, but better the devil you know…'

Joanna stared down at her plate, not daring to see what effect this implied criticism of his new fancy might be having on Gabriel.

However, he only sounded amused. 'Your tenant has demonic qualities?'

'Well, he wouldn't have been our first choice,' Charles said. 'We'd have preferred a couple to a single man, but at least the rent is guaranteed, and you can't have everything.'

Good God, Joanna thought blankly. They must be talking about Paul Gordon, the man I met this morning. So, he's actually living quite close by.

She was aware that her colour had risen suddenly, and, looking up, saw that Gabriel had noticed too, and was staring at her narrow-eyed. She took a hasty bite of a sandwich.

When tea was over, Charles asked Gabriel for a word of advice on a letter he'd had from his broker, and the two men went off together.

Joanna offered to help with the washing up, but was

quietly relieved when her hostess scoffed at the very idea.

Sylvia accompanied her out to the car. 'Don't be a stranger,' she said with mock severity. 'If life at the Manor gets you down, you can always use this as a bolthole.'

Joanna returned her heartening embrace, and drove away.

She hadn't really noticed the Lodge as she drove in, but now, as she approached it, she realised there was smoke coming from the chimney. As she slowed to negotiate the gateway Paul Gordon emerged from the front door and waved to her. She pulled over, and parked on the verge.

'Well, hello again.' He leaned in at the car window. 'I thought I caught a glimpse of you earlier. Obviously you know my landlords.'

'Yes, we're old friends. I've been having tea.'

He looked disappointed. 'Then I can't offer you a cup.'

'No, thanks.' She gave him a constrained smile. 'I have to be getting back, anyway.'

'But you will some other time?' He grimaced slightly. 'I feel a bit isolated, to be honest. The landlords were abroad when I moved in, and they haven't been all that sociable since their return.'

'Perhaps they feel they should keep any relationship on a business footing.' Joanna spoke coolly, disliking the implied criticism in his voice.

He groaned. 'Oh, hell, please don't freeze me too. I'm sure the Osbornes are really lovely people.'

'Indeed they are.' Joanna hesitated. 'Maybe we take slightly longer to make up our minds about people in the country.'

'Then I must be an inveterate townie,' he said

promptly. 'Because I knew I liked you from the first moment I saw you.'

She was aware of that tell-tale blush again, and angry with herself because of it.

She said sedately, 'Then that just shows the danger of snap judgements.'

'I'm not afraid of taking risks either,' he said. 'Which is something we have in common, Mrs Joanna Verne.'

'On the contrary.' Joanna put her car in gear, preparing to drive off. 'I'm extremely cautious.'

'Not if you plan to ride that chestnut on a regular basis.'

In the mirror she could see Gabriel's car turning the corner towards them, and cursed under her breath.

She said hurriedly, 'Actually, it's my husband's horse, so I doubt if I'll have much chance to take it out again. Now I really must go.'

'Of course.' He stood back from the car, his smile warm, lingering. 'But I look forward to seeing you again soon.'

He went back into the Lodge, closing the front door behind him. Joanna waited on the verge for Gabriel to overtake her. She half expected him to stop the car and make some comment, but he simply drove past— almost as if she hadn't been there, she thought crossly.

Yet she knew he'd seen her. Seen them. She'd felt his eyes boring into her all the way down the drive.

She followed at a safe distance until they reached the crossroads, when he took the road to Westroe instead of the turning to the Manor.

Off to Larkspur Cottage, no doubt, Joanna thought, cornering much too fast.

She straightened up, slowed down, and pulled over

to the side of the road. Killing herself, after all, wouldn't improve a thing.

It occurred to her that for the first time in her life she was experiencing male admiration from someone of her own generation. Apart from Gabriel, almost every man she knew was a contemporary of Lionel's.

Now she'd met someone who seemed to look at her as if she was a woman—and a desirable woman at that. And she wouldn't be human if she didn't find it flattering.

Paul Gordon was also attractive, she admitted. In some other lifetime she might even have been tempted to respond to his charm.

Instead, she thought wretchedly, she was trapped in her hopeless fixation on Gabriel. And much good that would do her.

Oh, why did it have to be like this? Why couldn't love be a kind and mutual thing, instead of a destructive force that swept you away into a hell of your own making?

And why was the person you wanted more than life itself destined to be always out of reach?

She sat, staring unseeingly through the windscreen, her throat aching with unshed tears, letting her mind turn in endless, empty circles.

And, when she could bear it no longer, she started up the car again and drove back to the Manor.

Back, she thought, to her cage.

She was met by an agitated Grace Ashby. 'The Persian rug from the morning room, madam. It's gone. Mrs Elcott's taken it to her cottage. And the porcelain candlesticks, and the set of Delft plates. A van came this afternoon while you were out, and collected them all.

'The two armchairs from the small sitting room have gone too, and all the furniture from Mrs Elcott's bedroom. It's been totally stripped, even down to the curtains. And she's got the Spode dinner service, and an entire boxful of household linen, not to mention ornaments, and Mr Lionel's snuff box collection...'

Joanna groaned inwardly. She said quietly, concealing her private dismay, 'Mrs Elcott has permission to take the things, Grace. Mr Gabriel said she could have whatever she wanted. I—I discussed it with him earlier.'

Although I didn't expect her to be quite so quick off the mark, she amended inwardly. Or so thorough.

'And I think you'll find everything's only on loan. The whole lot will be coming back to the Manor in due course.' Along with its new mistress, she added silently.

'Just as you say, of course, madam.' Mrs Ashby sounded doubtful. She paused. 'I understand neither Mrs Elcott nor Mr Verne will be dining at home this evening. Is there anything special you'd like?'

Just for a moment Joanna wondered if this was Grace Ashby's way of telling her that she knew what was going on, but a swift look at the other woman's patient, rather puzzled expression convinced her that she was wrong.

She said with an effort, 'I'm not all that hungry. Some clear soup and grilled fish would be fine.'

She bathed and changed into a plain grey woollen dress, long-sleeved and full-skirted. Its severe neckline needed some enhancement, she decided, taking out the pearls Lionel had once given her and clasping them round her throat.

Her solitary dinner over, she took her coffee into the drawing room. She switched on the television but found herself unable to concentrate on anything being offered on any of the channels.

She thought, I'll play some music.

Lionel had not been fond of what he termed 'gadgets', but he had invested in a handsome hi-fi system with a CD player, and they'd spent many companionable evenings listening to their favourite works.

Joanna made her selection from the rack of discs, and a moment later the emotive chords of Elgar's 'Cello Concerto' filled the room.

Curled up in a corner of the sofa, eyes closed, Joanna gave herself up to the poignant, dramatic flow of the music.

The final movement was reaching its climax when instinct told her that she was being watched.

Her heart began to thud. Slowly she opened her eyes and turned her head, to see Gabriel lounging in the doorway.

Joanna sat up hurriedly, searching for something—anything—to say, when she saw him raise a quiet finger to his lips, indicating that they should both be silent until the music was over.

When the room relaxed into stillness again, he came forward. He was smiling faintly, his brows drawn together in a slight frown. 'Do you always listen to such sad music when you're alone?'

'I don't know,' she returned stiltedly. 'Solitary evenings are a comparative novelty.' She paused. 'And I don't find it all that sad. I think it's powerful and—exhilarating.'

'I bow to your superior wisdom.' Gabriel removed his jacket and tossed it onto a chair, before seating himself opposite to her. He met her startled look levelly. 'Is something the matter?'

'I—I wasn't expecting you back so early.'

His frown deepened. 'Did I say I was going to be late? I don't think so.' He slanted a faint smile at her. 'Anyway, it means we can enjoy some domestic bliss together. Why don't you put some more music on?'

She said stiffly, 'Actually, I was on the point of going to bed.'

'Really?' His brows rose sceptically. 'Now, I got the impression that you were totally relaxed, lost in some world of your own.'

'Appearances,' she said, 'can be deceptive.'

'Ain't that the truth?' he murmured. 'But please don't let me drive you away. You never know. Music might prove the common ground where we can meet without quarrelling.'

'I doubt that exists.'

'Well, we can try. And for starters you could stop being so uptight.'

Joanna bit her lip. 'I'm—sorry. As I said—you startled me.'

'I don't know why. And I'm afraid, darling, you're just going to have to live with my arrivals and departures.'

She said coolly, 'I find the departures easier to handle.'

His mouth twisted, but he made no immediate reply. Instead the tawny eyes began a comprehensive survey of her, from the tendrils of soft hair brushing her flushed face, pausing momentarily at her exposed throat, then down over the cling of the grey wool dress to her rounded breasts, to the soft folds of the skirt outlining the slender length of her thighs. And back to her throat again.

He said softly, 'You look like a ghost—a little grey ghost. But my mother's pearls look good on you.'

'Your mother's?' Joanna's hand flew defensively to

the smooth string. 'I—I didn't know—Lionel didn't tell me...'

He shrugged. 'Why should he? He gave them to her when I was born. Under ordinary circumstances they'd have come to you anyway—probably to mark the birth of our own first child,' he added unsmilingly.

Her flush deepened. 'Then I'm wearing them under false pretences.' She put her hands up, fumbling for the clasp. 'You can have them back now.'

'Leave them,' he directed briefly. 'Pearls should be worn, or they lose their lustre.'

'My—successor might not agree with you.' Cynthia, she knew, had always coveted the necklace.

'Let that be my problem, rather than yours.' His tone brooked no further argument. 'Consider them on loan, if you wish.'

'After all, what's one more thing among so many?' Joanna muttered.

'I beg your pardon?' His brows lifted.

She said wearily, 'It doesn't matter,' wondering at the same time if he'd gone to Larkspur Cottage to oversee the disposal of his property.

'I'm going to have a nightcap.' Gabriel rose and went across to the antique corner cupboard. 'Care to join me?'

Prudence suggested she should refuse and go. On the other hand, she didn't want to seem altogether churlish...

She said sedately, 'Thank you. I'll have a brandy.'

He nodded. 'Then choose some more music for us to drink to.'

Joanna went reluctantly to the CD player. If he imagined she was going to allow this to develop into a cosy evening *tête à tête*, then he could think again.

Just because his rendezvous with Cynthia clearly hadn't worked out as planned…

A lot of the music was frankly too overtly romantic for the occasion. I need drama rather than passion, she thought, selecting Rimsky-Korsakov's 'Scheherazade'.

'Good choice,' Gabriel approved as he brought over their brandies. 'This has always been one of my favourites.'

'I—I didn't know.' Joanna cradled the brandy glass between her palms, breathing its heady aroma.

His mouth twisted. 'Music is just one of the many gaps in our knowledge of each other.'

He added another log to the fire and stood up, dusting his hands.

'I gather that's Charles and Sylvia's new tenant you were chatting to this afternoon.' He reseated himself and picked up his own brandy. 'Known him long?'

She shook her head. 'I met him just this morning.'

'You amaze me,' he said equably. 'I took him for an old and valued friend.'

She shrugged. 'Perhaps one relates to some people more quickly than others.'

'Clearly one does.' His tone mocked her formal phraseology, and she stiffened. 'As a matter of interest, how did you meet him?'

'I wouldn't have thought it was a matter of any interest to anyone except ourselves,' she said coolly.

'Then you'd be wrong.' He studied the colour of the brandy. 'While we remain married all your acquaintances—fascinate me.'

She hesitated. 'I met him this morning while I was riding. He was walking along Wellow Lane.' She paused, mentally skating over the exact circumstances of their meeting. 'We—got into conversation, that's all.' She threw him a challenging look. 'Is there anything wrong in that?'

'You tell me,' Gabriel murmured.

'Or,' she went on, 'has some ban been imposed on my making friends at all?'

'Not in the least.' He took a meditative sip. 'What's his name?'

'Gordon,' she said with exaggerated clarity. 'Paul Gordon. If it means anything to you.'

'Nothing,' he said. 'And I'd like to keep it that way.'

She stared at him. 'Meaning?'

'Meaning I'm sure I can rely on you to behave with discretion.' His tone was silky.

Joanna put her brandy down on the sofa table with a bang that threatened to shatter the fragile crystal.

'My God.' Her voice shook. 'Congratulations, Gabriel. You've just elected yourself king of the double standard.'

'Meaning?' He turned her own question against her.

'Meaning your own record wouldn't stand up to close scrutiny,' she flung back at him.

'Harsh words, sweetheart. On what do you base this assumption?'

'Your rake's progress has been well documented,' Joanna said scornfully.

'Gossip columns,' he said, 'are not the most reliable sources—whatever they themselves believe.'

'Are you saying you've passed the last two years in total celibacy?'

His mouth tightened. 'No. When you're hungry, Joanna, you'll take whatever crumbs are available.'

Her voice shook. 'And your appetite is naturally prodigious.'

He gave her a thoughtful glance. 'I'm sure you always thought so.' His sigh was brief and harsh. 'Yes, I've strayed, but not seriously, and not often. Is that what you wanted to know?'

'Your love life is no concern of mine.' She could feel the pulse hammering in her aching throat. 'But the lady who follows me may take a different view.'

'I hope so,' Gabriel drawled. 'I really couldn't face another battery of wifely indifference.'

Joanna got to her feet, outraged. 'You—you hypocrite,' she said unevenly.

It was you, she thought, who was indifferent. You who didn't care—who left me here, bleeding to death.

He rose too. 'More harsh words?' His voice bit. He walked over to the CD player and silenced it. 'Perhaps I should teach you some manners.'

'Take some lessons yourself—in fidelity,' she hit back at him.

'Oh, I've already learned that, my love.' His smile seemed to grate across her shivering skin. 'My bride-to-be will have nothing to complain about, I promise.' He laughed harshly. 'Isn't it amazing what love can do?'

The pain that consumed her was intense. From some reserve of strength she hadn't known she possessed she managed to raise her head. To smile, even.

She said, 'That's not something I feel qualified to judge. But—to return to Paul Gordon—I'll be discreet if you are, Gabriel. And that's all I'll guarantee. So it's up to you. Goodnight.'

She turned towards the door. He reached her in two strides, his fingers closing like a vise on her shoulder.

'Joanna—listen to me...'

'Go to hell.' She glared at him. 'And take your hands off me.'

Behind them the drawing room door opened quietly.

'My goodness,' Cynthia purred, her narrowed eyes flickering over them. 'Is this a private fight, or can anyone join in?'

Joanna flashed her a glittering smile. 'It's the end of round one.' Her voice sounded brittle. 'And I'm ahead on points.'

Head high, she left the room, shutting the door behind her. Closing them in together. As she crossed the hall she could hear the murmur of voices, and Cynthia's tinkling laugh.

The bravado seemed to ebb out of her suddenly. She leaned against the newel post, staring unseeingly into space.

What price one hollow victory? she asked herself wretchedly. When the war is already lost? And you know it.

And, slowly and defeatedly, she began to climb the stairs towards the loneliness of her bedroom.

CHAPTER EIGHT

'THE decorator has finished, and my new bed should be delivered tomorrow,' Cynthia said complacently. 'So I can move into the cottage later this week.'

She smiled at Joanna across the breakfast table. 'Which will be much more convenient—for everyone. Don't you think, my pet?'

'If you say so,' Joanna agreed quietly, frowning over her post.

'It looks very nice now that it's all been painted. I probably wouldn't have bothered, as I don't plan to stay there very long, but Gabriel insisted.' Her smile widened. 'He's incredibly considerate—in every way.' She sighed nostalgically, then put her head on one side. 'Why don't you pop down this afternoon and have a look at the cottage? It is your property, after all.'

'I'd almost forgotten,' Joanna returned with cool irony. 'And I'm afraid I'm busy this afternoon. I promised Mrs Barton I'd help at the hospice shop.'

Cynthia's eyes glinted maliciously. 'Still maintaining the fiction that you're the Lady of the Manor, darling? I wonder what penance you'll have to do for deceiving the vicar's wife.'

Joanna folded her napkin and rose. 'Don't worry, Cynthia. Living in this house, under these conditions, is penance enough for all the sins of the world, believe me.' She gathered up her letters and left the room.

In the hall, she paused, drawing a deep, steadying

breath. How much more, dear God, was she supposed to take?

The past fortnight had been a nightmare. She had felt all the time as if she was tiptoeing on thin ice. Since their last confrontation Gabriel had treated her with cool civility, and she had tried to respond in the same way.

During the daytime she'd done her best to keep out of the way. It was Gabriel who now rode out with Sadie first thing in the morning, while Joanna deliberately postponed her own ride until later in the day. She even delayed coming downstairs in the morning, to avoid encountering him at the breakfast table.

But some meetings at mealtimes were inevitable, and she'd been forced to observe Cynthia's blatantly proprietorial attitude towards him—the hand on his sleeve, the whispered asides, the teasing, pouting looks.

She could only be thankful that neither of them chose to dine at the Manor very often, and that they spent their evenings together at the cottage—the lack of the new bed being apparently no deterrent.

Joanna bit her lip. She couldn't afford to think on those lines, she adjured herself firmly. She had to stay detached—impersonal. It was the only way.

She looked down at the letters in her hand. But for once it seemed as if her avoidance policy would have to be temporarily abandoned. Because she needed to talk to Gabriel.

With a sigh, she crossed to the study door and knocked, waiting for his terse 'Come in' before entering.

As he registered who it was his expression became closed, almost wary.

He rose formally to his feet. 'Joanna—this is an unexpected pleasure.'

She heard the question in his voice—the surprise. And another note, less easy to analyse.

He looked tired, she thought, his eyes shadowed, the lines on his face strongly marked. But then she recalled the reason for his faintly haggard appearance, and hardened her heart against a pain that went too deep for tears.

She said coolly, 'Don't worry. This isn't a social call.' She put the letters she was carrying on the desk. 'I'm beginning to get requests from local people—organisations. The Red Cross want to know if they can hold their usual garden party here in July. The Riding Club are asking us—you and I—to present prizes at the gymkhana. The list is growing, and I—I don't know what to tell them.'

'Because of our personal circumstances?' His tone was ironic.

She nodded. 'It seems wrong to—pretend that everything's fine and normal, when...' Her voice tailed away.

Gabriel sighed sharply. He picked up the letters. 'Would you like me to deal with these?'

'Thank you. That might be best.' She gave him a fleeting, wintry smile, and turned away.

'Jo—wait.' The harsh urgency in his tone halted her in her tracks.

'Is something wrong?'

He said grimly, 'Just about everything, I'd say. Will you sit down for a moment, please? We need to talk.'

She paused, then took the chair by the fire, perching tensely on its edge.

'What is it now?' She lifted her chin. 'More rules for me to obey? I've tried to follow your regime.'

'I'm sure you have.' He was silent for a moment. 'The fact is, Joanna, it was never feasible—for either of us. Sharing a roof like this is an impossible situation.'

She was very still. 'As I've tried to tell you.'

'Indeed you did.' He bent his head almost defeatedly. 'So I'm looking for a way out—for both of us. I thought you'd want to know.'

'Yes,' she said, dry-throated. 'Yes, I'm—very grateful.' She hesitated. 'May I know what's made you change your mind?'

It was Gabriel's turn to pause. He said reluctantly, 'Let's say I've had time to think. And I've been made to see how unfair this situation is to you.'

In other words, pressure from Cynthia, she thought with a pang. She told me herself she wasn't planning to stay long at the cottage. No, she wants to take over here, and for that she needs to be rid of me.

Aloud, she said, quietly, 'So—what do you suggest?'

'I don't know yet. There are all kinds of ramifications that need going into thoroughly.' The tawny eyes were sombre. 'But I'll make sure you don't suffer, Jo.'

Ah, but I am suffering, she cried out in silent anguish. More than you can ever know. Because, although living here has been purgatory, leaving—never seeing you again—will be the worst kind of hell. And how will I bear it?

'Thanks again.' She got to her feet. Her voice was bright. 'It will be good to make some plans at last—to decide what to do with the rest of my life. I'm sure you feel the same.'

His mouth twisted. 'My plans are already made. All I need is the freedom to carry them out.'

'Yes,' she said. 'Yes, of course.'

He said, 'So that's that. Shall we shake hands on a bargain?'

Startled, Joanna hesitated, then slowly put her hand into his.

A half-forgotten line of poetry came into her mind. '"Shake hands for ever, cancel all our vows."'

But it wasn't until she saw his brows lift in mocking acknowledgement that she realised she'd spoken aloud.

He said, 'Ah, but remember how it starts, Joanna.' He quoted softly, '"Since there's no help, come let us kiss and part."'

She looked up at him mutely, mesmerised by the sudden intensity in his tawny gaze. Then he bent his head, and gently, even tentatively, put his mouth on hers. He did not take her in his arms, or try to impose any other intimacy upon her. It was a breath of a kiss, a sensuous brushing of lips, hauntingly sweet, but with a kind of sad finality. It drew them into a tiny, shaken vortex of feeling. Held them rapt, in total thrall to each other, motionless, deaf and blind. Until some slight sound—a log, perhaps, crumbling in the grate—made them draw apart.

Gabriel was breathing rapidly, the warmth in his eyes turned to a dangerous flame.

His voice was low, savage. '"Nay, I have done: you get no more of me."' He threw back his head in an oddly defensive gesture. 'You'd better get out of here, Joanna.'

Without another word, she obeyed.

The hospice shop was only open on a part-time basis, so it was invariably busy.

Joanna, asked to take charge of the nearly-new

clothing section, found herself too occupied to brood—a blessing in itself. But the memory of that kiss and its aching sweetness stayed with her like a shadow, no matter how hard she tried to put it from her mind.

She'd left the study and gone straight up to her room, remaining there until she was sure that Gabriel, and then Cynthia, had left the house.

But when she was alone, the house seemed strangely oppressive, and she'd taken the dogs up onto the hill. It was a cold, clear day, and she'd sheltered from the wind by the Hermitage stones.

She'd looked down at the Manor, standing below her, absorbing every detail, imprinting it on her memory for all the long, lonely days ahead. Saying goodbye for ever.

Then she'd walked slowly back, changed, and driven into Westroe, pale but composed, for her stint at the shop.

Towards the end of the afternoon, she was approached by a harassed Mrs Barton.

'Mrs Verne, could you possibly stay on and lock up for me? My husband's just rung to say that Sarah's fallen and hurt her wrist, and one of us should take her to Casualty.'

'Oh, poor kid.' Joanna grimaced sympathetically. 'You go straight away. I'll cope.'

'That is good of you.' Mrs Barton rolled expressive eyes at the ceiling. 'Children—there's always something.' She patted Joanna's arm. 'As you'll soon find out, I expect.'

Joanna felt the smile freeze on her lips. So many people blithely assumed that she and Gabriel were reconciled, she thought unhappily. They were the focus of a lot of genuine goodwill.

She only hoped that he would find a solution to their problems soon, and release her from this treadmill of other people's expectations. And her own unfulfilled longings, she thought with a little sigh.

As closing time approached Joanna cashed up, and then took some unwanted carrier bags and packing materials out to the dustbins at the rear of the shop, then went into the little curtained changing room to retrieve some dresses which had been tried on but not purchased.

'Well, I think it's a proper scandal.' It was the tart voice of Mrs Golsby, one of the regular helpers and an inveterate gossip. 'He must be years younger than she is, and he's round there at that cottage with her all the hours God sends. I feel heart-sorry for Mrs Verne,' she added self-righteously, and there was a brief murmur of assent from her two colleagues. 'It can't be nice for her—her own stepmother carrying on like that.'

Joanna shrank into the corner of the cubicle. It was what she'd feared. Gabriel's affair with Cynthia was becoming common knowledge. But, as a result, her own departure wouldn't cause quite as many shock waves, she reminded herself without pleasure.

She tiptoed back into the rear passage, then came back noisily, rattling the clothes hangers she was carrying. She gave the other women a smiling goodnight, as if she didn't have a care in the world, and watched them leave.

Then she hung the discarded dresses back on the rail, and bent to take the shop keys from their hook under the counter. As she did so the doorbell tinkled.

Joanna straightened. 'I'm sorry. I'm just closing. We'll be open again on Friday,' she began, then stopped abruptly.

'I know.' Paul Gordon smiled at her. 'I've been hanging round outside for ages, waiting for you to shut up shop.'

'Why?' Joanna stared at him.

'Because I spotted you when I was passing earlier, but you were obviously too busy to interrupt.' He paused. 'So I decided to let the rush die down, then ask you to have dinner with me.'

'That's very kind of you.' Joanna was taken aback. 'But I couldn't possibly.'

'Why can't you?'

'For all kinds of reasons. We hardly know each other.'

'And we never will, if you keep turning down my invitations.' He looked at her with a half-smile. 'So what's the problem? Do you have to rush home like a good little wife to dish up your husband's dinner?'

'No,' Joanna returned, nettled. She already knew she was destined for another solitary meal tonight. Unless...

Paul Gordon was not what she wanted, and never would be, but as that was beyond her reach anyway, why shouldn't she take him up on his offer?

With which slightly muddled reasoning she accepted. 'All right. I'd like to have dinner. Shall I go home and change, and meet you later?'

'You look fine to me. And this—' he indicated his jeans, roll-neck sweater and elderly tweed jacket '—is as good as it gets. My wardrobe down here is strictly limited, I'm afraid. But I'm told the wine bar in the High Street doesn't operate a strict dress code.' He gave her a hopeful look. 'And perhaps we could go for a quiet drink first. Get acquainted.'

In spite of herself, Joanna was amused. 'You have the whole evening planned, I see.'

'Not all of it,' he said softly.

Joanna caught an audacious gleam in the blue eyes and knew a flicker of misgiving, which she firmly crushed.

She said, 'I'll get my coat.'

They went for a drink to the White Hart. Paul ordered beer for himself, but could not talk Joanna out of her request for a mineral water.

'I'm driving,' she reminded him. 'But I'll have a glass of wine with the meal.'

He was an amusing enough companion, she was forced to admit. He seemed to have had a variety of jobs, including writing advertising copy and working in some minor production capacity for an independent television company.

'There aren't many media opportunities round here,' Joanna remarked lightly.

'Which is probably a good thing.' Paul wrinkled his nose. 'Because it's freed me for the serious bit. I started a novel some time ago, and now I've got an agent and a publisher definitely interested, so I've come down here to finish it in peace and quiet.'

'I thought you were looking for a social life,' Joanna remarked, sipping her mineral water. 'Yet writing's supposed to be a solitary occupation, isn't it?'

He shrugged expansively. 'Well, of course. But I don't intend to devote every waking moment to it.' He smiled at her with what she felt was conscious charm. 'You know what they say about all work and no play.'

He paused. 'But that's enough about me. Tell me about you. Was that your husband who passed us the other afternoon? He looked rather fierce.'

'His father died last month,' Joanna said quietly. 'It's not a particularly joyous time—for either of us.'

'God, I'm sorry.' He looked genuinely remorseful.

'You weren't to know.'

'Have you been married long?'

Hardly at all, thought Joanna. Aloud, she said, 'Three years, but Gabriel's been away much of the time. He has a very successful investment company.'

'And you don't accompany him on his travels?' The blue eyes sharpened. 'How can he let you out of his sight?'

Joanna looked down at her glass. 'We have an arrangement that works,' she said. She forced a smile. 'I'm getting hungry. Shall we go and see what the wine bar has to offer?'

They reached it down a flight of stone steps. It was a long room, with a polished wooden floor and a low ceiling. One wall was taken up with wine racks, and a blackboard displayed the day's menu, which seemed to specialise in seafood.

Joanna decided on sea bass, with scallops wrapped in bacon to start, while Paul chose game terrine, followed by steak.

He wanted to order two bottles of wine, one white and one red, to complement their respective meals, but Joanna hastily dissuaded him, saying firmly that one glass of the house white would suffice for her.

He seemed disposed to argue the point, so she excused herself and went to the women's cloakroom.

She looked reasonable, she thought, viewing herself critically in the big mirror above the basin. Not glamorous or exciting, but reasonable. She was wearing a flared black skirt, with the new cream silk shirt, and a patchwork waistcoat in jewel colours.

I seem like someone about to have dinner with an

attractive man, she thought detachedly. That's if you don't look too deeply into my eyes. And as long as he doesn't expect too much.

I ought to have watched Cynthia, of course. Observed the body language. Practised that husky note she puts into her voice.

Although Paul Gordon might then think she was marginally interested in him, and that simply wasn't the case.

Except that he puzzled her slightly, she amended inwardly. He claimed to be a struggling writer, yet while his shabby clothes bore out his claim, his wallet was brand-new, and stuffed with money.

And the dogs, she remembered suddenly, hadn't liked him.

She gave herself a wry glance as she turned away. Was she simply inventing a mystery to get her through what could prove to be a sticky evening? Very probably. Well, she would eat her dinner, thank him nicely, and make sure their paths didn't cross again.

When she got back to the table the wine had been served, and the waitress was just bringing their first courses.

It was easier once the food arrived. It was good, so it could be praised, and reference made to likes and dislikes, and other meals enjoyed elsewhere. Far safer topics than any further interrogation over the state of her marriage.

The main course had been brought, and the vegetable dishes were being placed on the table, when the outer door opened, bringing in a sudden gust of cold air.

Joanna glanced up casually, then stiffened in incredulity as Gabriel came into view. Eyes widening, she

watched him slip off his overcoat and hang it on the
rack by the entrance before walking across to the bar.
Judging by his reception, he was clearly a regular and
valued customer.

Of all the gin joints in all the world, she thought
dismally. Although he had to eat somewhere when he
wasn't at the Manor, she supposed, and Cynthia was
certainly no cook.

'Is something wrong?' Paul leaned towards her at-
tentively.

She shrugged. 'It seems my husband has decided
to dine here tonight as well.'

'Oh.' His head turned sharply in the direction of
the bar. 'Is this going to be a problem for you?'

'Not in the least.' She gestured at her plate. 'This
sea bass is delicious.'

'He's seen us,' Paul muttered. 'He's coming
across.'

He was already beside them. 'Joanna—what a de-
lightful surprise.' His drawl was pronounced. 'Won't
you introduce me to your companion?'

She acquiesced reluctantly, making them known to
each other in a small wooden voice.

'Won't you join us?' Paul asked expansively.

'Thank you, no. I'm expecting a guest myself.' He
looked down at Joanna. 'You didn't tell me you were
dining out tonight, darling?'

'That's because I didn't know. It—was a last-
minute thing. Paul happened to be passing the shop,
and we found we were both at a loose end.'

And why was she embarking on this string of explanations, as if she needed to justify herself, when
Cynthia would no doubt be arriving in the next few
minutes?

Perhaps it was because of the undercurrent of anger that she sensed in his cool, almost languid tone.

But what the hell did he have to be angry about, anyway? she wondered, deliberately needling herself. She was the one with the right to be mad. The right to get her own back.

'At a loose end?' Gabriel sounded meditative. The smile he directed at them both was charming. 'A dangerous situation for a wife to be in. Maybe I should make sure that your every moment is fully occupied in future, my sweet.'

Joanna's fork clattered on her plate. She kept her voice level. 'But for that you'd have to be around far more often than you are, Gabriel. And you know how boring that would get.'

She picked up her glass and drank, hoping the cool wine would assuage the burn in her throat.

'Then I'd have to make sure it was worth the sacrifice.' Gabriel's voice was light, but there was a note in it which sent a shiver across her nerve-endings. 'Enjoy what's left of your meal, both of you.' And, with a nod, he walked away back to the bar.

'Oh, dear,' Paul commented, *sotto voce.* 'I think you could be in trouble, Mrs Verne.'

'Nonsense.' Joanna spoke stoutly, helping herself to more broccoli. Out of the corner of her eye she could see that Gabriel was using the public telephone at the end of the bar. Warning Cynthia to delay her arrival, no doubt, until they had completed their meal and departed.

She found herself wondering, vengefully, if it was possible to make a pudding and a pot of coffee last until the wine bar closed.

But Gabriel would soon see through that ploy, and extricate himself with another phone call. And it would also mean several more hours in Paul's company, a prospect which she didn't particularly relish, although she'd have been hard put to it to say why.

He was clearly exerting himself to be pleasant. In his own book, she supposed, he hadn't put a foot wrong. Yet there was just—something which didn't gel.

He was almost too smooth. His answers seemed too pat, as if he'd done a crash course in the responses she'd find acceptable. And that was ridiculous.

I'm the problem, she thought, putting down her knife and fork with regret. Maybe this is how the dating game works, and I'm just not used to it.

'Is that all you're going to eat?' He looked at her plate with concern.

'I'm not as hungry as I thought.' She forced a smile. 'Do you think we could get the bill and go, please?'

'Yes, of course.' Paul signalled to the waitress.

In whose wake came Gabriel again. Joanna found her hands balling into fists in her lap. She made herself unclench them, and reach for her glass instead.

'Leaving already?' He sounded all concern as he watched Joanna swallow the last of her wine. 'Shall I phone for a taxi to take you back to the Manor, darling?'

'No, thanks. I have my car.' Her tone was terse.

His brows lifted. 'But do you think it's wise to drive—when you've been drinking?'

Her smile back at him was saccharine-sweet. 'One glass of wine with a meal? I don't think that would trouble the breathalyser, do you? And Paul's promised to make me an enormous pot of black coffee at his place, anyway, so—there's really nothing to worry about.' She got to her feet. 'Do enjoy your meal,' she added. 'I can recommend the sea bass.'

And, without a backward glance, Joanna walked to the door and out into the night's dark chill, which she recognised because it already shivered in her heart.

CHAPTER NINE

'YOU can be a powerful woman.' Paul caught up with Joanna in the street, his tone a mixture of surprise and admiration.

'When the occasion warrants it.' She felt in her bag for her car keys, aware that her hands were shaking.

'I suppose I should have known,' he went on. 'When I saw you mastering that horse the other day.' He paused. 'What a shame you no longer have the chance to ride it.'

'You have an amazing memory for detail.' She sent him a tight-lipped smile. 'I'm sorry for the premature ending to our meal. It was—most enjoyable.'

'But it doesn't have to end here. You told your husband you were coming back to my place for coffee.' He gave her a persuasive look. 'I hope you're not going back on your word.'

Her heart sank. 'I wasn't really serious about that...' she began.

'Well, I am,' he said firmly. 'Besides, you don't want him to find out you just went tamely home, as per instructions, do you?'

Actually, Joanna thought, that was none of his business. Her lips were parting to tell him so when another car turned the corner into the High Street and pulled up outside the wine bar with a squeal of brakes.

Turning, Joanna saw Cynthia climb out of the driving seat and walk across the pavement with a click of high heels.

She felt as if she'd swallowed an enormous stone

which had become lodged in her midriff. And the fact it was exactly as she'd expected made no difference at all.

She looked up at Paul Gordon. 'No,' she said evenly. 'That's the last thing I want. And I'd be glad of some coffee. I'll fetch my car and follow you, shall I?'

'I'll have the coffee brewing,' he promised, and went off jauntily.

Joanna turned, and began to walk in the opposite direction. The impulse to keep going until she fell off the edge of the world was a strong one.

She was developing a headache, if she was any judge, and all she wanted to do was drive home, take some paracetamol and fall into bed. And decent oblivion.

Spending another hour or more in Paul Gordon's company, and drinking coffee too, would do nothing to improve her physical well-being or her temper. And it was all Gabriel's fault, she thought, lashing herself on to the next stage of vindictiveness.

Because anger was so much easier to deal with than hurt and heartbreak. And soon those would be all that was left to her.

The Lodge was lit up like a Christmas tree when she got there. But that was better than a continuation of the wine bar's intimate candlelit ambience, she decided sourly, parking her car.

As she reached the door it opened, and Paul was there smiling at her.

'I'd begun to think you weren't coming,' he chided playfully.

Shrewd of you, Joanna thought, recalling the ten

minutes she'd spent sitting in the High Street car park, fighting with herself.

She said lightly, 'I'm a woman of my word.' Not to mention a prize idiot and a stubborn mule, she thought as he helped her off with her coat.

The living room at the Lodge wasn't big, but it had been nicely decorated and furnished by the Osbornes, with a sofa and an easy chair covered in dark green flowered chintz and a paler green carpet.

She glanced around her with genuine pleasure. 'This is really cosy. So, where do you do your writing?'

'I thought the table in the window.' He grimaced. 'My computer's still packed away in boxes, I'm afraid.'

She looked at him in faint surprise, having gained the impression his novel was in full swing.

She said, 'I understood publishers imposed all kinds of deadlines.'

'I'm probably not important enough for that. Not yet, anyway.'

'I'm sure it's only a matter of time,' she said tactfully, aware it was the response he wanted. Playing him at his own game, she realised wearily.

He disappeared into the kitchen and came back with a tray laid with pottery mugs, a cream jug and a cafetière.

Whatever reservation she might have about him, his coffee was excellent, and she complimented him sincerely, causing him to launch into a monologue about the exacting art of the choosing and blending of beans.

Were all would-be writers as self-obsessed as this? Joanne wondered with faint amusement.

She'd deliberately chosen the chair to maintain her

own space, and was annoyed when he fetched a leather pouffe from a corner and established himself at her feet.

'That's better.' He smiled up at her.

'And that's a matter of opinion,' she returned under her breath, debating with herself how soon she could leave. She would have to finish her coffee at least, and it was too hot to gulp down.

She looked at the painting over the mantelpiece. 'Is that one of Sylvia's?'

'Possibly. I'm not really into amateur daubs.'

That was the kind of thing Cynthia said, and she stiffened. 'I don't think either of those terms applies to Mrs Osborne's work.'

'I'm sorry.' He didn't sound repentant. 'But I'm just more used to shows at the Hayward Gallery. That is, if you want to talk about art. Now, I'd rather talk about you.'

For a writer, his dialogue could use a little work, she thought judiciously.

'A very boring topic.' She kept her tone light.

'Not from my viewpoint. I find you quite fascinating.'

'I don't know what can have led you to that conclusion.' She took a gargantuan swallow of coffee.

'Perhaps I'm just more perceptive than most of the men you've known. For instance, it's obvious your marriage is going nowhere.'

'Unlike myself,' Joanna said thinly, and put down her mug. 'Thanks for the coffee, Paul, but I really must be leaving. I'll see myself out.'

She made to rise, but he stopped her, a hand on her knee.

'Don't be silly, sweetheart. And stop pretending. We both know why you're here. That dog in the manger act of his didn't fool me for a minute. He neglects you, and you don't deserve it.'

She said icily, 'Will you please allow me to rise?'

He laughed. 'What a coincidence. I was just going to ask you the same thing.' His hand pushed at her skirt, stroking the slender nylon-clad thigh.

She tried to hit him, but he captured both her fists in his other hand and held her, still laughing.

'Playing hard to get? You don't have to. I know the score, and I'm very discreet. Just relax and enjoy yourself.'

She said between her teeth, 'Not with you,' and kicked him hard. She connected with his shin and Paul gasped and swore, releasing her to clutch at his leg.

Joanna was on her feet in an instant, and making for the door. As she reached the hall he caught her, turning her to face him.

'What the hell's the matter with you?' It was good-bye to Mr Smooth. 'You knew what to expect when you came back with me. You've been begging for it ever since I first saw you.'

'Like hell I have,' she flung back at him, twisting to free herself from his clutching hands, wondering what the hell she was going to do if he persisted. As it seemed he might...

She saw him lean towards her, his mouth moist and parted, his eyes hot. And heard, like the answer to a silent prayer, someone knock loudly at the front door. She thought, Gabriel—oh, thank God...

'Joanna?' It was Charles Osborne's voice. 'Joanna, are you there, my dear?'

Paul Gordon muttered an obscenity, but his hands fell away from her.

Joanna snatched her coat from the rack and marched to the door, flinging it open.

'Charles.' In spite of herself, her voice quivered a little. 'What are you doing here?'

'Saw your car outside.' Charles stepped into the hall. 'Good evening Mr—er,' he added as an after-thought, then turned to Joanna again. 'Sylvia was wondering if you'd like to come up to the house for a nightcap?'

Joanna swallowed. 'That's—very kind, but I was just on the point of going home. Another time, per-haps.' She looked at Paul, who was standing red-faced and sullen. 'Goodnight, Mr Gordon.'

The door slammed shut behind them. 'Funny sort of chap,' Charles observed as they walked to her car. 'Can't make him out, really. Can't say I trust him.'

'Don't worry about it,' she advised curtly. 'He isn't worth the trouble.' She paused. 'Charles?'

'Yes, my dear?'

She bit her lip. 'I suppose Gabriel asked you to do this—rang you from the wine bar?'

'Not a bit of it,' he denied, too promptly. 'Noticed your car as we drove in. Thought you might fancy a drink, that's all.'

She smiled at him, but inwardly she was smarting. 'Charles, you're a terrible liar, but I forgive you. Give Sylvia my love, and tell her I'll ring her soon.'

'Sure you're all right to drive home?' He sounded troubled.

'I'm fine,' she lied. 'No problem.'

In reality she was shaking like a leaf, inside and out. Falling apart.

She drove back to the Manor with exaggerated care, and went straight to her room.

She ran herself a bath, stripped, and submerged in

the hot water, washing every inch of herself as if she
were contaminated. In reality, of course, Paul Gordon
had hardly touched her, but her skin felt as if it was
crawling.

When she'd stopped trembling, she got out of the
water and dried herself. She didn't dress again, but
instead put on a housecoat she rarely wore, which had
been part of her trousseau. It was dark green velvet,
full-skirted, with long tight sleeves and dozens of tiny
buttons down the front.

She had given her hair a rough towelling, and now
the pale tendrils curled softly round her face. Her
cheeks were flushed, her eyes hard and bright. She
thrust her feet into the little embroidered mules which
matched the housecoat, and sat down in the armchair
by the fire.

She resisted the temptation to stretch out on the
bed, because she was afraid she might fall asleep. And
it was imperative that she stayed awake and waited
for Gabriel to come back. There were things she
needed to say to him—at the top of her voice, if necessary. Her life could not go on as it was. Somehow
she needed to clear away the morass of anger, wretch-
edness and confusion inside her.

Common sense told her he might be gone all night,
but if so, she thought, lifting her chin, she would be
ready to face him in the morning.

But she wasn't asked to go to these extremes after
all. It was barely an hour later when she heard his car
come up the drive and stop.

She put aside the book she had been trying to read
and stood up, aware her legs were trembling. For the
first time it occurred to her that he might not have
returned alone—that Cynthia might be with him.

She went across to the door and stood listening intently. But there was no sound of conversation, and the footsteps that ascended the stairs and passed her room were solitary ones.

She stood for a while, composing herself and marshalling her thoughts, then let herself quietly out of her room and walked along the passage.

She turned the handle on his door, and went in. The room itself was empty, but the bathroom door was ajar and she could hear taps running. Gabriel's jacket and the rollneck sweater he'd been wearing earlier were both lying across the bed.

She hadn't set foot in this room since she'd helped Mrs Ashby get it ready for him. But in that short space of time he'd made it wholly his, she thought, looking round.

His brushes were on the dressing chest, and beside them a pair of gold cufflinks which Joanna recognised. They were the ones she'd given him on their wedding day. She touched them gently, aware of faint surprise that he still had them, let alone used them. She'd have thought that he'd jettison them, along with all the other unhappy memories.

'Make yourself at home.'

She turned, startled, to find him standing in the bathroom doorway, watching her, a towel slung over one bare shoulder.

'I presume you've come for a fight,' he went on. 'Fine—let battle commence.'

She stiffened. 'I'm glad you find it so amusing.'

'You're wrong. I find it tragic.' Hands on hips, he looked her up and down critically. 'But I approve your choice of armour. Is it new?'

'No,' she said. 'I've had it for three years.'

Gabriel winced theatrically. 'Ouch. First blood to

you, darling. But I'm sure you're not here merely to demonstrate what I've been missing.'

Joanna's hands balled into fists, concealed by the skirts of her housecoat.

'No,' she said. 'I'd like to know what the hell you meant by sending Charles round to the Lodge tonight.'

'I suppose I thought you might be glad to see him. Was I wrong?'

No, damn you. She managed somehow not to say the words aloud. Knowing how accurately he'd gauged the situation only added fuel to her anger.

She said icily, 'Completely and totally wrong.'

'Then I apologise.' He sounded unruffled. 'I thought, you see, that you'd only agreed to go back with him to annoy me. And that once he'd served his dubious purpose you'd appreciate being rescued.' His smile was faintly contemptuous. 'I hope I haven't spoiled a beautiful friendship.'

'Not at all.' She lifted her chin. 'It's only the first of many. And in future I can do without your unwarranted interference.'

'In that case I hope you'll choose your next—friend with slightly more discrimination.' He shook his head. 'Gordon isn't good enough for you, Jo.'

'How dare you say that?' Her voice shook. 'Considering your own choice of partner...'

'I don't expect you to approve.' He shrugged. 'But believe me when I say she's everything I've ever wanted in a woman.'

Pain made her hollow. Made her want to hurt him back.

She raised her eyebrows, parodied his drawl. 'Then your standards must have slipped dramatically, my dear Gabriel.'

His mouth twisted. 'In your eyes, I never had any standards anyway.' He slung the towel across a chair. 'To hell with this, Jo. Do we have to go on sniping at each other?'

'Not at all,' she said. 'As long as you acknowledge I have the right to live my own life, and form whatever relationships I please.'

'And does Paul Gordon please you?' There was faint mockery in his tone.

'Yes,' she lied. 'Yes, he does.' She even allowed herself a small, reminiscent smile. 'Very much. If that's any concern of yours.'

Gabriel's face was expressionless. 'We're still married, Jo.' He paused. 'And I don't want you to be hurt.'

For a moment Joanna stared at him, stunned. He could still say that, after everything that had happened between them? After the humiliation of letting her see that he didn't want her—that their marriage was a trap from which he couldn't wait to escape? After staying away for two years without contact of any kind?

Not to mention the even greater misery of knowing she was going to be replaced by her own stepmother.

She took a deep breath. She said thickly, 'I don't know which I despise most, Gabriel. Your arrogance or your hypocrisy.'

His head went back as if she'd struck him, but when he spoke his voice was level. In control. 'Well, you won't have to endure either of them for much longer. I talked to Henry Fortescue tonight, and we worked out a deal for you.'

'What kind of a deal?'

'I've agreed to pay you myself the yearly sum that Lionel specified in his bequest. And an additional sum for maintenance. The arrangement can commence as

soon as you wish.' He paused. 'I'm afraid I can't include Larkspur Cottage—or not immediately, anyway.'

'No,' she said, her lips suddenly numb. 'No, of
course not.'

'Henry's going to draw up the necessary paper-
work,' he went on. 'When it's completed, and signed,
you'll be a free woman.'

'And the divorce?'

'I've told Henry to set that in train too.' His glance
was a challenge. 'Satisfied?'

She bit her lip. 'This is very—generous of you.'

'On the contrary. I'm as anxious to be rid of this
situation as you are.'

She said slowly, 'I—appreciate that. I hope we
can—part friends.'

'Now who's being a hypocrite?' His voice lashed
at her. 'We've come a hell of a way from friendship,
Joanna.'

'Why are you so angry?' She stared at him. 'You—
we've both got what we wanted.'

He said slowly, 'Because anger is a much easier
emotion to deal with than some of the alternatives I'm
experiencing right now.'

The room seemed to have shrunk suddenly, the
walls closing in on her. Although Gabriel hadn't taken
a step, she felt him near to her. So near that if she
put out a hand she could touch him. Could feel the
warm silk of his skin under her hands. The clean,
male scent of him, at once achingly familiar and ter-
rifyingly alien, seemed to fill her nose and mouth, so
that she breathed him, absorbed the essence of him
into her inmost being.

Her breasts pushed against the cling of the velvet,
her hardening nipples excited by the delicate friction.

Under the flowing skirt her legs were weak, the secret female core of her burning, molten.

His eyes were pools of gold, glowing like the eyes of a sleek jungle cat watching its prey.

Except that she could turn and run away right now, and he would not follow.

Only she would not run—this time.

She could sense the tension in him—the arousal—because she shared it.

Instinct drove her. Her voice was low, husky. 'Tell me about them, these emotions of yours.'

He shook his head slowly. 'You might not want to know.'

Her smile, faint, oblique, challenged him. 'Try me.'

He said softly, 'Is curiosity an emotion, Joanna, or a deadly sin? Because I'd die to know if you're wearing anything under that pretty green gown of yours.'

She moved a shoulder almost diffidently. 'Not a thing.'

'Ah,' he said. 'Now, how long would it take, do you think, to undo all those little buttons?'

'I haven't the slightest idea.' Her hand went to the top one, released it from its loop. 'Do you want to time me?'

A ghost of a laugh shook him. 'No—just to watch.'

She didn't hurry. She watched him in turn—the flare in his eyes, the sudden heat spreading along his cheekbones. She heard his intake of breath as the edges of the pliant velvet fell apart.

For the first time in their life together she was revealing herself to him, and the power of it made her almost dizzy.

She shrugged the gown from her shoulders, held it for a moment, bunched round her hips, then let it fall completely.

The silence in the room—the stillness—was charged, pulsating.

Then Gabriel moved, covering the space between them in two strides, sinking on his knees before her, putting his cheek then his mouth against the flatness of her belly in an act that seemed like worship.

He said, with a kind of desperation, 'Oh, God—do you know—have you any idea how truly beautiful you are?'

She put out her hand, touched the springing darkness of his hair.

He drew her gently downwards so that she was kneeling in front of him. As he kissed her her lips parted for him in longing and surrender. His hands were stroking her, feathering down her spine, moulding every slight, graceful curve, and she felt her body arch towards him in blind delight. He cupped her breasts in his palms, bending his head to kiss them, to caress the eager rosy peaks with his tongue, making her sigh with pleasure. With need. One sensation seemed to blur into the next, so that she hardly knew when he lifted her to her feet, and into his arms, to carry her to the bed.

Through half-closed eyes she watched him strip off his trousers, but when his hands went to the band of his briefs, she stopped him.

'Let me do that,' she whispered.

He lay beside her as she gently freed him from that last constraint, his head pillowed on his folded arms, the lambent tawny eyes devouring her.

'I should have mentioned,' he said lazily, watching the direction of her own widening gaze. 'That other emotion was lust. Definitely a deadly sin.'

'Somehow I guessed.' She touched him shyly, her fingers tracing the power of his virility until he gasped

and rolled towards her, imprisoning her under one
muscular thigh.

'I'm sorry.' She looked up at him, stricken. 'Did—
did I do something wrong?'

Gabriel laughed softly. 'Quite the opposite. You
were doing everything right, but I don't want to lose
all my control just yet.'

He began to kiss her slowly, deeply, sensuously,
his tongue grazing hers. His hands caressed her blos-
soming breasts, teasing the tumescent nipples into a
pleasure that bordered on pain.

His mouth suckled her. His hands caressed her, exploring every curve and plane, inventing new sensa-
tions, making every inch of her come alive, each
nerve-ending sing.

She pressed herself against him, gasping, her lips
busy with small, frantic kisses against his skin.

His fingers discovered the delicate flesh of her inner
thigh, lingered there, moved on her sweetly and rhyth-
mically, making the breath catch in her throat.

She heard a small, strained voice she barely recognised as her own say, 'Oh—there. Please—there.'

Every nerve-ending, every atom of her being was
concentrated on that tiny point of feeling he was revealing to her.

Her head turned from side to side on the pillow,
her breathing rapid and shallow. Her hands gripped
his shoulders, trying to draw him down to her. Into
her.

'Gabriel.' His name was a plea. 'Oh, God—*Gabriel*...'

'No.' He breathed the word against her skin. 'No,
darling—not yet. This is for you—only for you.'

She was poised for ever on the edge of some vortex. She could hear herself whimpering. Then pleasure

imploded in her, her body clenching deliriously in wave after wave of piercing sweetness.

Reality returned slowly, and with it a sense of well-being—of completion that she'd never experienced before.

She opened her eyes. Gabriel was sitting beside her, one leg drawn up and his forehead resting on his bent knee. There was a faint sheen of sweat on his back, and she put out a languorous hand and touched it.

He jumped, as if she'd used her nails.

She said with a new shyness, 'Gabriel—darling…?'

'Yes, my sweet?' The endearment, and the smile which accompanied it, seemed almost perfunctory.

For a moment she felt chilled, but told herself it was sheer imagination.

She said, 'I—I didn't know it could be like that.'

'Didn't you?' His smile was almost mocking. 'Well, I suppose I have been rather remiss in the past where your sexual education was concerned.' He picked up her hand and dropped a careless kiss on the palm. 'But you're an apt pupil, darling.'

She hadn't imagined a thing. Suddenly she was shivering.

'What are you talking about?'

'This little crash course in female response that we've just enjoyed.'

'Is that what it was?' Her mind didn't seem to be working properly. Nothing made any sense. '*All* it was?'

'I hope,' he said, 'that you weren't disappointed.'

It hurt to breathe. 'No—but I—I thought we were going to make love.'

'That wouldn't be very wise—under the circumstances.' The tawny eyes glittered at her. 'Besides,' he added, shrugging, 'we'd need to practise safe sex, and unfortunately I'm not equipped for it tonight.'

She tried to laugh, but it sounded more like a sob. 'You make it sound so—clinical.'

'Experiments usually are. But I'm glad this one was so successful.'

'Are you?'

'Oh, yes,' he said lightly. 'After all, I can't have you going to some stranger without knowing what turns you on.'

'No,' she said quietly. 'I'm sure your pride wouldn't allow that.' She looked down at him, her brows lifting. 'I see it's replaced lust as the current deadly sin.'

He yawned. 'And will soon be overtaken by sloth, I fear. Do you want to stay here, or would you prefer to go back to your own room?'

She kept her voice steady. 'Thank you, I'd rather sleep in my own bed.'

She slid to the floor and walked to where her velvet housecoat lay in a crumpled heap, aware all the time of his eyes watching her.

She pulled the garment on, her hands clumsy as she huddled it round her, and started for the door.

From some far distance she thought she heard him say her name, but she didn't even falter.

Pride, she thought as she got outside, wasn't just a deadly sin. Sometimes it was all there was to cling to, in the wreckage of your hopes and dreams.

Head bent, she walked quickly down the passage. She had just reached her own door when something— some sound—some movement—attracted her attention.

Cynthia was standing at the head of the stairs, staring at her, an unpleasant smile twisting her lips.

She said, 'Well, well, Joanna. I hope you haven't been making a fool of yourself, my pet.'

Without speaking, Joanna went into her room.

And sometimes, she thought wretchedly, as she closed the door and leaned back against its panels, even pride was taken away from you.

She stood where she was for a long time, staring across the room at the reflection in her mirror. It was someone she didn't recognise at all—a stranger, half-naked, with dishevelled hair, and tears pouring endlessly down her white face.

CHAPTER TEN

IT WAS nearly dawn before Joanna finally fell into a restless sleep. She simply lay there, staring into the darkness, her eyes tearless at last, and burning, trying to make sense of what had happened but failing utterly.

Gabriel had wanted her. There was no question about that. Nor had he made any attempt to hide it. But then, suddenly, he had no longer wanted her, and she'd been dismissed from his bed—and from his life.

A situation with which she was all too familiar. And yet she'd still allowed it to happen.

It's all my own fault, she thought, pressing a fist to her mouth as her whole body cringed in pain. I asked for it—talking about divorce one minute and throwing myself at him the next.

She supposed that he'd remembered, just in time, that he was committed to Cynthia now. That he intended to make the relationship work.

I should have been the one to remember. The one to step back, she told herself. I can't say I wasn't warned. Now I have to live with the consequences.

Starting this very morning, she realised, hugging herself defensively.

She wanted to stay in this bed, with the covers pulled over her head, but what remnants of pride that still remained wouldn't allow her to take the coward's way out.

Pride made her shower and dress and go downstairs with her head high and every line of her body a challenge. But, to her unspoken relief, she had the dining room to herself.

Perhaps this morning Cynthia had kept Gabriel with her, to make amends for last night's minor transgression.

But she couldn't think about that, she told herself, as she drank orange juice and coffee, and crumbled some of the freshly made toast that Grace insisted on bringing.

She would think about the new life ahead of her. The freedom which had been placed so unexpectedly within her grasp and which only she would know was an illusion.

When the world was your oyster, it was strange how small and bleak it suddenly became.

Everything she wanted in life was here under this roof, and she had to detach herself and walk away. Wasn't it the mandrake plant that was said to scream when pulled up by its roots?

I hope I have more dignity than that when the time comes, she thought. But I don't guarantee a thing.

When she'd finished her pretence at breakfast, she went to the stables, where Sadie was mucking out, her face glum.

'What's the matter?' Joanna fetched Minnie's tack and began to saddle up.

Sadie did not meet her enquiring gaze. 'Jimmy and I were in the Royal Oak last night,' she mumbled at last. 'And everyone was talking, Jo. Saying what's going to happen here. Made me feel quite sick.'

Joanna braced herself. 'I presume they were talking about Mr Verne—our divorce...'

Sadie looked aghast. 'No, no one mentioned... Oh, Jo, it isn't true—surely? Not that on top of everything else?'

Minnie shook her head and moved restively, as if aware that her mistress was not concentrating on the job in hand. Joanna quieted her with a soothing word and a hand on her glossy neck.

She kept her voice cool and level. 'I thought it would have been obvious the way things were going. Tongues have certainly been wagging in Westroe.'

'Then that must be why Mr Gabriel's decided to sell up and move,' Sadie said miserably.

'Sell up?' Joanna echoed in disbelief. 'What on earth are you talking about? Gabriel would never sell the Manor.'

Sadie looked at her mournfully. 'That's what they're all saying, Jo. It's those Furnival Hotels people again—the ones who wanted Mr Lionel to sell to them a couple of years back.'

'Yes, but he saw them off.' Joanna fastened Minnie's girth with hands that were shaking. 'Told them he wasn't interested and never would be.'

'But he's not here any more,' Sadie said unanswerably. 'And it stands to reason that Mr Gabriel doesn't feel the same way about the place, or he wouldn't have stayed away all that time. And if there's going to be a divorce too...' There was a short, heavy silence. 'They reckon he's going to sell out to Furnivals and move back to London. I was sure you knew all about it.'

'I'm clearly not as well-informed as the Royal Oak.' Joanna tried to find a grain of humour in the situation and failed. The ground seemed to be shaking under her feet. 'Who's the industrial spy?'

Sadie bit her lip, looking evasive, and Joanna suddenly remembered that Debbie Macintosh, the landlord's daughter, worked in Henry Fortescue's office.

She said, rather grimly, 'On second thoughts, I'd rather not know.'

She began to lead Minnie over to the mounting block, and heard Nutkin whicker softly as they passed.

What would happen to the horses? she wondered with anguish. And they were the least of it. There was Grace and her husband, Sadie, and the rest of the people who worked on the estate. All part of a safe, secure world shortly to be blown out of the water.

The dogs, she thought numbly. I could at least keep the dogs. Cynthia's never liked them, and they'd hate the city.

But I can't leave it there. Maybe—somehow—I can talk to Gabriel—convince him not to do this. Make him see this is his birthright—his inheritance—and he has a duty to it.

Only he wouldn't listen. Perhaps he'd intended this all along. Casting off the old shackles for his new life—his new wife. Making any sacrifice she wanted.

And, let's face it, Cynthia would rather queen it in London and New York than play Lady of the Manor. It was probably all her idea.

And the fact that Gabriel had been prepared to listen only proved how much he loved her.

Joanna swung herself up into the saddle, looking down at Sadie's bent head as she tightened Minnie's girth.

Sadie said forlornly, 'Do you think the hotel people will keep the stables on?'

'I don't know,' Joanna said gently. 'But please remember this is only a rumour. It may never happen.'

'They were saying the Furnival people are coming down soon to talk over a deal.'

Joanna patted Minnie's neck. 'And I say Debbie

had better learn to be more discreet if she wants to keep her job,' she returned drily, and rode out of the yard leaving Sadie gaping after her.

It was a grey morning, but milder than it had been, and Joanna turned Minnie's head towards the hill.

When she reached the Hermitage she dismounted, tethered Minnie to a stump of tree, and sat down on a fallen rock.

Below her, the house looked as it always did, as if it had evolved naturally out of the landscape. As she'd imagined it would always look, whether or not she was here to look after it.

The Furnival chain had produced grandiose plans for its development, she remembered unhappily. Tennis courts, a health spa and swimming pool. Lionel had heard them out in silence, then dismissed them with icy finality. She'd thought that would be the end of it.

But I should have known they wouldn't give up so easily, she told herself bitterly, wondering just how soon after Lionel's death they'd made their move. But they'd regard that as business—just another deal. And perhaps that was how Gabriel saw it too. After all, he was just as ruthless. He wouldn't let sentiment stand in his way either. Or the transient desire of a moment.

When she had come up here to say goodbye the previous afternoon, it had been on a purely personal basis. She would leave, but the Manor would endure. She had not foreseen—how could she?—just how all-encompassing that farewell might be.

At least, she thought sombrely, she would never be tempted to return.

Minnie, grazing quietly, lifted her head and whinnied sharply. Joanna, startled, turned her head and saw Paul Gordon standing a few yards away.

She got slowly to her feet and stood watching him, her head thrown slightly back, her gaze cool and unwelcoming. He wasn't dressed for open country, she thought critically, observing his tight-fitting denim jeans, his black leather jacket and the cream silk scarf wound round his throat.

He, however, seemed perfectly pleased with himself, and totally unabashed. 'I was hoping I'd run into you.'

Joanna pushed her hands into her pockets. 'The pleasure is entirely yours.'

'How unkind,' he said lightly, 'when I did my best to show you a good time.' He paused. 'However, I accept that I allowed my ardour to get the better of me, and I want to apologise.'

'Ardour?' Joanna's brows lifted.

'Of course,' he said. 'You're a very lovely, clearly neglected girl. You surely can't blame me for trying?'

No, Joanna thought. Not if I believed you. But I didn't get the impression you were carried away by overwhelming passion. On the contrary, the whole situation seemed strangely orchestrated. But, then, what do I know?

She shrugged. 'Let's just agree we both made a mistake and forget about it. The chances are we shan't meet again, anyway.'

His smile was ingratiating. 'But I wouldn't want us to quarrel.'

'That's hardly likely.' Joanna lifted her chin. 'We don't know each other well enough.'

'That could change.'

'Not,' she said, 'in my lifetime.'

He laughed. 'Cold little devil, aren't you? No wonder the handsome husband prefers to warm himself at a different fire.'

Even as the jibe went home Joanna, wincing inwardly, saw movement on the hill behind him. A gleaming chestnut gelding was picking his way towards them across the tussocky grass, his rider sitting easily in the saddle. Her heart missed a beat.

For a moment the thought that Gabriel might have guessed where she'd gone and followed played crazily in her mind. But it was as quickly discarded. His appearance on the hill was just a coincidence, but one that she could use to her own advantage. She was damned if she was going to leave him with an image of her depressed, lonely and isolated. She would try a little orchestration of her own.

Deliberately, Joanna walked to where Paul Gordon was standing, running a hand lightly up his arm to his shoulder.

She dropped her voice to a throaty drawl. 'Perhaps you're right. Maybe that's what I need too.'

She saw suspicion in his face, warring with his natural egotism, but self-love won. For a very long moment, which made her soul writhe, Joanna endured the touch of his mouth on hers.

As she freed herself and stepped back she saw Gabriel go past at the canter, his face dark and hard, as if carved from obsidian, the amber eyes not sparing them a glance.

Paul Gordon saw him too. The gratified smirk vanished and his brows snapped together. 'What the hell...?'

'Don't worry about it,' Joanna said kindly. She went over to Minnie and released the rein.

His eyes narrowed unpleasantly. 'I do believe you were using me, you little bitch. And I don't like that.'

'You mean you'd much rather believe you were irresistible?' Joanna swung herself up into the saddle, shaking her head as she looked down into his angry face. 'Not to me, I'm afraid.'

He reached up to grab for her rein, but Minnie threw up her head and sidled away from him.

'Or to dogs and horses, apparently,' Joanna said, clicking her tongue reprovingly at the muttered piece of filth he directed at her.

'I'll make you sorry for this.' His tone was venomous.

'I think not.' Joanna said coldly. 'Because I already deeply regret becoming even marginally involved with you.'

She turned Minnie, and rode off in the opposite direction to that which Gabriel had taken.

She didn't look back, but she was aware of Paul Gordon's furious gaze boring into her back as she departed.

Sylvia and Charles had been fully justified in their reservations about him, she thought, urging Minnie to a canter when they reached level ground. Under the mask of charm, Paul Gordon was a nasty piece of work.

In spite of her troubled thoughts, she found she was enjoying her ride. There were signs of spring all around her—evidence of a new beginning which she should maybe see as an omen for her own life. Which could help her clarify the direction she should take.

Down in one of the hollows, where a small stream pushed its way between rocks, she found a cluster of primroses, and picked a few to push into her buttonhole while Minnie drank from the cold rush of water.

Joanna watched her fondly. Min had been the first horse she'd ever ridden, sure-footed and dependable even then, and she was good for plenty of years in the future, providing she found a good home.

And it's up to me to see that she does, she told
herself with renewed determination. So, when I get
back, I'll set the wheels in motion—about this, and a
few other things as well. Think positive.

As she guided Minnie back up the slope the mare's
ears went forward, and she whinnied eagerly.

'What's the matter?' Joanna held her firmly. 'What
have you heard?'

As she reached the crest she saw the reason for
Minnie's excitement. Gabriel was waiting for them in
the middle of the track, his face enigmatic under the
peak of his hard hat.

'Good morning.' His tone was cool and formal.

'Good morning,' Joanna returned. She felt a wave
of betraying colour rise in her face and bent forward
to adjust one of Minnie's straps to hide it. 'I—I
thought you'd gone the other way.'

'I came round in a circle.' His gaze strayed to the
pale yellow blossoms in her buttonhole. 'I guessed
you'd come here. It was always one of your favourite
places.'

Which he knew, she thought, because he himself
had shown it to her, back in the old, innocent days
when he'd been not merely her angel but her god. A
very long time ago.

'I'm sorry if I spoiled your tryst earlier,' he went
on.

'Please don't apologise,' Joanna said coolly. 'I'm
sure there'll be others.'

'As you say.' Nutkin danced a little and was swiftly
controlled. 'Maybe next time you should choose a less
obvious place.'

'Probably,' she said. 'But then I haven't your experience in these matters. Perhaps I could come to you
for some tips.'

His face was like stone. 'I don't recommend it.' He
paused. 'But do me one favour, Joanna. Delay the
consummation of your fling until after the divorce.'

Joanna lifted her chin. 'For what reason?'

'A very practical one. You could become pregnant
and if you were still technically my wife, it could
throw up all kinds of problems.'

'Practical indeed,' she agreed expressionlessly.

And also bloody impossible, she wanted to scream
at him. Because I wouldn't touch Paul Gordon if he
were the last man on earth—even before he let the
mask slip.

Because the only man I want to father my child is
right here in front of me now, God help me.

Aloud, she said, 'Then perhaps you'd allow me a
favour in return.'

'If it's possible. What do you want?'

I want you, she thought. Now, and for all eternity.

She said, 'I'd like to take Minnie with me, when I
go.' She paused. 'And I want you to sell me Nutkin.
I gather from Sadie you're not going to keep him
yourself.'

Gabriel's brows lifted in undisguised surprise.
'You're going to have your own stable?'

'Eventually.' She nodded. 'And in the meantime I
can keep them at a livery.'

He said drily, 'You seem to have it all worked out.'
He was silent for a moment. 'Of course you can have
Minnie, but I'm not sure about Nutkin. He's not easy
to manage—even for me.'

'Nevertheless, I'd like to try. I think we belong together, Nutkin and I.'

His mouth twisted. 'I'd like to know what you base
that on.'

Both of us outsiders. Neither of us wanted around any more.

Aloud, she said, 'Instinct, I suppose.'

'That's not enough. You'd need to prove to me you could handle him.'

'Are you saying I don't ride well enough?'

'On the contrary,' he drawled. 'You had an excellent teacher.'

'Yes,' she said, deliberately misinterpreting his words. 'Lionel had endless patience.'

He winced elaborately. 'What ingratitude. And hardly the way to gain a favour.'

She shrugged. 'I haven't agreed to yours yet, either.'

Something came and went in his face. For a moment the atmosphere shimmered with tension. But tension laced with some other element, which Joanna sensed but could not analyse. The horses felt it too, and began to move uneasily.

Joanna watched Gabriel quieten Nutkin with effortless assurance. Horses had always been such an important part of his life, she thought desolately. How could he contemplate a life without them in London? Did he really believe Cynthia was worth this kind of sea change in his existence?

Across the space that divided them, their eyes met. He said quietly, 'But I hope you will.'

'*Quid pro quo*, Gabriel. One good turn deserves another.'

His smile was wintry. 'I'm not sure I'd describe Nutkin as a good turn. But if you show me you can ride him, then I'll give him to you.'

'I said I'd buy him,' she reminded him.

'We've settled the broad basis for our separation,' he said wearily. 'For God's sake, let's not fight over trivial details. I've given you little enough during our ill-starred relationship. Just take the bloody horse, will you?'

'May I take him now? Prove to you I can stay on him?'

'It isn't the right saddle for you.'

'All the same.' She tried to smile. 'I want the deal done—before you change your mind.'

'It's not something I make a habit of.'

No? she wanted to scream at him. Then what was last night about?

But that, of course, she could never say.

Instead, 'I hear you've changed your mind about staying at the Manor,' she said as she slid off Minnie's back.

Gabriel's head turned sharply. 'What the hell do you mean?'

She shrugged. 'I gather Furnival Hotels are back in the picture.'

'They're preparing an offer.' He turned his attention to the stirrup leathers he was shortening.

She swallowed. 'Which you mean to accept?'

'Which I mean to consider.'

'Oh.' She was silent for a moment. 'I can't believe you'd do that.'

'Why not?' His tone was matter-of-fact. 'It's a valuable piece of real estate.'

'But it's your home.'

'Not for the past two years.' His gaze rested ironically on her flushed face. 'And absence doesn't always make the heart grow fonder.'

'I—see.'

'I doubt very much that you do,' he returned shortly. 'In any case, it's none of your business—

apart from the sum from the sale that would become due to you under the divorce settlement.'

She gasped. 'You really think I'd accept—blood money like that?'

'I suspect that's something that our respective lawyers will decide.' His drawl became more pronounced. 'And it's hardly blood money. I didn't kill anyone for it.'

'But you're destroying the house. Turning it into something it was never meant to be. Ripping the heart out of a family home and everyone who works for it and supports it.'

'My God, Joanna,' he said softly. 'Such vehemence. Perhaps you should go into politics.'

She said between her teeth, 'And maybe you should go to hell.' She put a foot into the stirrup, swung herself onto Nutkin's back, and took off.

She heard him shout after her, telling her to stop, to wait for him. But she took no notice. Just sat down in the saddle and let the horse run.

She needed to distance herself. To come to terms with the fact that, as he'd said, it was none of her business. No longer her house. No longer her home. Separate ways. Separate lives.

Anyway, it occurred to her that she'd probably already used up any reserves of his goodwill there might be. So what did she have to lose?

Nutkin carried her like a dream, strong, effortless and eager.

'You and me against the world,' she shouted into the wind. She tried to laugh, but the laugh cracked in her throat and turned into a sob.

They were nearing the Hermitage. It was time to slow Nutkin and turn for home. She glanced over her shoulder, but Gabriel wasn't even in sight.

As she turned back again she saw it. Ahead of them. Something white, billowing out on the breeze from between the fallen stones. She knew in the same split second that Nutkin had seen it too. Felt his muscles bunch and heard his frightened squeal as he reared.

And saw the ground coming up to meet her as she fell.

CHAPTER ELEVEN

THERE were faces, swimming in and out of her vision. Usually she could put names to them, but not always. There were voices, too, which seemed to come from the bottom of some deep sea. And words that she recognised, like 'slight concussion' and 'nothing broken.'

Which didn't stop her whole body feeling like one enormous bruise, even against the softness of her bed.

She forced her eyes open, searching for one particular face. Found it stark and grey with shock. She wanted to hold his head between her hands and kiss away the nightmare from his eyes, but she couldn't. Because he didn't belong to her. She couldn't even tell him that she loved him, promise that everything would be all right.

Instead, she heard her own voice, oddly small and strained, say, 'You mustn't blame Nutkin. It wasn't his fault.'

And his bitter response. 'You could have been killed, Joanna, and all you can think of is that bloody animal.'

The doctor intervened at this point, saying that she needed rest and quiet, and that it might be better to move her to a local nursing home where these could be guaranteed.

'No,' Joanna said, with all the force she could summon. 'No, thank you. I—I want to stay here. I'll be fine.'

She couldn't bear to be sent away, even for her own

good. As if something—some inner voice—warned that once she left, she would never return. That this would serve as an excuse to distance her for ever.

The faces round the bed retreated. The voices faded and she was alone, cocooned in a soreness that couldn't even touch the all-encompassing ache in her heart.

She swallowed the painkillers the doctor had left and settled back against her pillows, seeking the promised oblivion.

She dozed eventually, but restlessly, dreaming of pounding hooves, the wind in her face, and that billowing gleam of whiteness which had ended it all with such dramatic suddenness.

White fabric, she thought feverishly, flowing all around her, wrapping itself across her face so that she couldn't see—so that she couldn't breathe...

She sat up with a little cry, wincing as her bruises protested at the sudden movement.

What was it? she asked herself. What on earth could it have been?

'So you're awake.' Cynthia spoke from the doorway. She was wearing a woollen suit in deep crimson, the collar and cuffs trimmed with fur, and her lips and nails were painted to match her suit. She looked like some exotic but poisonous flower. 'I just came to say goodbye. I'm moving into my cottage as from now.'

She surveyed Joanna's white face and shadowed eyes with undisguised malice. 'You look like hell, sweetie. And all for nothing. Or did you think Gabriel would be impressed with your dramatic attempt to break your neck?'

Joanna stared at her. She said slowly, 'Are you implying I came off on purpose? Because it's not true.

Something spooked Nutkin. Something white floating about between the rocks near the Hermitage.'

Cynthia's lips curled. 'Another runaway newspaper, perhaps? You have a vivid imagination, my dear. Not that it matters.' Her laugh jarred tinnily. 'All you've accomplished is to embarrass Gabriel and damage a valuable horse.'

'Nutkin's hurt?' Joanna asked sharply. 'What's the matter with him?'

Cynthia shrugged. 'How should I know? Something to do with one of his legs, I think. Anyway, the vet's coming later to put the wretched animal out of its misery.'

'No.' The word burst out of Joanna. 'No, he can't do that. It can't be that bad.' She threw back the covers and shuffled painfully to the edge of the bed. 'I've got to see Gabriel—talk to him.'

'Gabriel's gone out, my pet. I really don't think he could bear to stay in the house with you. I've never known him so angry.' She studied an imaginary fleck on one immaculate nail. 'But I could always give him a message for you when I see him. Naturally he'll want to make sure that I'm safely settled in.'

Joanna bit her lip. 'He'll need to be here when the vet comes. I'll talk to him then.'

'Oh, well—if you're determined to humiliate yourself even further.' Cynthia shook her head. 'Poor, confused Joanna. You just don't know how to give up gracefully.'

She turned and went out of the room. The scent she was wearing remained, hanging heavily in the air, making Joanna feel faintly nauseous.

She limped doggedly into the bathroom and filled the tub, adding a generous handful of herbal bath salts. Getting into the bath wasn't easy, but the hot

water welcomed and soothed her, and gradually he
shaking body began to relax.

She dried herself carefully, patting the towel ove
her bruises, and put on fresh underwear. The firs
outer garment that came to hand was the green velve
housecoat, which she dropped as if it had suddenly
burst into flames. Instead, she chose a simple navy
jogging suit. Safe and sexless, she thought, zipping up
its tunic top to the throat.

Then she brushed her hair back from her face and
secured it at the nape of her neck with an elastic band.

'The doctor said you had to rest.' Grace Ashby met
her grimly at the foot of the stairs. 'And I don't know
what Mr Verne will say.'

Joanna's heart missed a beat. 'Is he back?'

'Just this minute. He's making a phone call before
he goes down to the stables. He's expecting the vet.'

'Yes—yes, I know.' Joanna took a deep breath.
'I—just want a word with him first.'

The study door was ajar, and she could hear no
sound of conversation. Joanna pushed the door fully
open and went in. Gabriel was standing with his back
to her, staring out of the window. He gave the impression of someone who'd been there for an eternity.

As she entered he swung round, and she remembered what Cynthia had said about his anger.

There was a coldness in him which reached out and
touched her, freezing her to the bone.

'You wanted something?'

'I need to tell you what happened on the hill. Why
I fell. Because it wasn't Nutkin's fault.'

She paused, searching his face, but it told her nothing. Biting her lip, she ploughed on. 'He has one fault,
but I think I could cure it. He freaks at white fluttering
things. And there was something among the fallen

stones at the Hermitage. The wind caught it, and blew it towards us, and it frightened him.'

His look was sceptical. 'What kind of something?'

'I don't know. It's all still confused, but I think it was a piece of material.'

'Oh, for God's sake,' he said, his tone a mixture of derision and bitterness. 'Your loyalty to that bloody horse astounds me. You'll go to any lengths to make excuses for him.'

'I'm just protecting my property.' She straightened aching shoulders. 'I want you to know the deal still stands—and send the vet away.'

He said roughly, 'The horse is a rogue, Joanna. I haven't forgotten what happened to my father. And this morning you could have been killed too. Although it would have been your own fault,' he added grimly. 'How dared you go off, hell for leather, like that?'

'Because I wanted to prove I could ride him. And I did. Nutkin getting spooked again was just un-lucky…'

'Oh, stop it, Joanna.' His voice bit. 'I found you, remember, and there was no material blowing in the wind, white or any other damned colour. Just you in a crumpled heap on the ground and that fool of a horse dancing round you.' He threw back his head and looked at her, his face oddly haggard, a muscle working beside his mouth. 'I thought you were dead.'

She forced her mouth into a travesty of a smile. 'Yet here I am—alive and kicking in spite of it all. And begging you to give Nutkin another chance—with me. Please don't let the vet put him down.'

'Put him down?' There was genuine astonishment in his voice. 'What are you talking about? He's got a strained tendon, that's all. I want the vet to take a look at it.'

'But I thought…' Joanna began, then stopped. So it had all been just another piece of Cynthia's malice, she realised bitterly. And not something that Gabriel would want to know about. Eventually, she supposed, he would find out what the woman he loved was really like.

He can't live in Cloud-Cuckoo-Land for ever, she thought painfully. But he's not going to hear the truth from me.

'What did you think?'

She shrugged. 'I knew you weren't impressed with him, and I heard he'd been injured, so I put two and two together and made thousands. I'm sorry.'

Gabriel nodded abruptly. 'I can't make an immediate decision about our deal. I'm still not happy about it.' He paused, a small, hard smile playing about his lips. 'But you make out a good case, Joanna. Maybe it's a pity I'm not a horse. You might have given me another chance too.'

And he went past her out of the room, leaving her staring after him, one hand pressed to her trembling mouth.

'You could have been killed,' Sylvia said reproachfully.

It was the following day, and the older woman had arrived for coffee and 'a look at the walking wounded', as she put it.

Joanna sighed. 'I know. It was a genuinely stupid thing to do, and I've no defence.' She paused. 'I was just so—needled by everything that I didn't stop to think. To weigh the consequences.'

'Well, we've all done that,' Sylvia said comfortably. 'But not usually on the back of an edgy thoroughbred.'

'No,' Joanna admitted. 'Anyway, it was good of Gabriel to tell you what had happened, and very kind of you to come over.'

'Nonsense,' Sylvia said robustly. 'Naturally, I'm concerned about you both.' She put down her coffee cup and studied the younger woman with a frown. 'You're still very pale. How are you feeling?'

'Stiff as a board,' Joanna said with a grimace. 'But that's what a close encounter with the hill does for you.' She hesitated. 'And it worries me that I can't remember much between coming off Nutkin and finding myself back here.'

'What does the doctor say?'

'To stop worrying and let nature take its course.' Joanna's brows drew together. 'I can remember someone bending over me at some point.'

'Well, that would be Gabriel, of course.' Sylvia gazed pensively at her rings. 'I gather he carried you down here.'

Joanna bit her lip. 'So I believe,' she said neutrally. 'But it isn't just the accident. I have this feeling that there's something I should remember—something that's been said to me since that's important.'

'Oh, that's maddening.' Sylvia directed a searching look at her. 'Could it be to do with whatever needled you into your headlong flight? May I know what that was?'

Joanna's expression was troubled. 'It's pretty much an open secret. I'd heard that Gabriel's planning to sell the Manor to Furnival Hotels.'

'I think the possibility exists.' Sylvia nodded. 'But why should the idea upset you so much?'

Joanna gasped. 'You—of all people—to ask that.'

She gestured around her. 'This is his home—his heritage.'

'It's certainly a beautiful old house, or Furnivals wouldn't want it,' Sylvia said drily. 'I think Gabriel's attitude to it is rather more ambivalent.'

'What do you mean?'

Sylvia considered for a moment. 'You speak of it as his home. Well, it hasn't provided much of a home life for him over the past three years—and I'm not apportioning blame here,' she added quickly. 'Gabriel's no angel, and never has been.'

'Yes, but all that is going to change.' Joanna's voice sounded small and suffocated. 'Once we're divorced.'

'Divorce causes a pretty dramatic change in peoples' lives,' Sylvia agreed. 'As to the heritage point— Gabriel has no son to whom he can hand on the estate, nor any likelihood of one.'

Joanna made a business of refilling the coffee cups. 'But that's not necessarily true,' she said with constraint. 'When he remarries…'

Sylvia shook her head. 'Not so. He's entirely ruled out the possibility of having a family. He told me so himself. So you can see why his inheritance no longer has much relevance for him. A home without children becomes simply—a house.'

Joanna mechanically busied herself with the cream jug, her mind whirling.

How could Gabriel possibly have accepted such a drastic denial of a basic human need? she asked herself. Cynthia was still a comparatively young woman—and, anyway, having children in the late thirties, and older, had become a commonplace these days. If there was some physical problem, there was a whole range of treatment for which Gabriel could easily afford to pay.

Or did Cynthia simply not wish to be burdened with the responsibility?

Whatever, it confirmed once more the depth of Gabriel's feeling for her, if he was prepared to forgo fatherhood for her sake.

She said, half to herself, 'What a terrible—tragic waste.'

'I agree,' Sylvia said levelly. 'But he's totally adamant. It grieves me to say it, but I think he can't get rid of the place quickly enough.' She paused. 'I understand that your stepmother has finally moved out?'

'Yes. She's now living at Larkspur Cottage.' *And Gabriel didn't come home last night, indicating that, to all intents and purposes, he's moved in with her.*

'Well, I hope she proves a more reliable tenant than ours,' Sylvia said tartly. 'He's just given notice, right out of the blue.' She snorted. 'Not that Charles and I are sorry. Engaging young men with no visible means of support are not favourites of ours.'

Joanna frowned, glad that the conversation had shifted to a less personal and thus less painful topic.

'But he's a writer, isn't he?'

Sylvia gave her an old-fashioned look. 'I believe he tells some such story. But his rent is paid by the local social security office. Not that he allows that to cramp his style particularly,' she added austerely. 'Crates of wine, and hampers of food from Fortnum's and Harrods. Nice work if you can get it.'

'But how can he afford that if he's unemployed?'

Sylvia's smile was cynical. 'We imagined he had someone else to foot his bills.' She paused. 'At one point we were afraid it was going to be you.'

'Because I had dinner with him once?' Joanna

asked. 'For which he paid—or at least I thought he did.'

'I expect the cheque is still bouncing.' Her gaze was shrewd. 'Not sorry to see him go, I hope, my dear?'

'On the contrary.' Joanna remembered the mean, pinched expression on the good-looking face. The veiled threat. 'We didn't part on good terms.'

'What a relief,' Sylvia said robustly. 'Although I told—' She stopped, looking dismayed, then rallied. 'But it's not important.'

Joanna forced a smile. 'You told Gabriel precisely what, Sylvia?'

Sylvia sighed heavily. 'That you had far too much sense to be taken in by such an obvious fraud.'

'Thanks,' Joanna said, with something of a snap. 'It would be good if everyone would stop treating me like a child.'

Sylvia drank the rest of her coffee and replaced the cup in its saucer. She said quietly, 'But isn't that what you've always wanted, Joanna? Firstly from Lionel and later from Gabriel. To be a little girl, petted and protected, instead of a woman?'

'Is—that really what you think?' Joanna was stunned.

'It's the impression you've given.' Sylvia reached for her bag and rose. 'Perhaps Gabriel is right, after all. Perhaps you do need to get away from here—to find your own space and stretch your wings. To realise your full potential.' Her smile was kind and sad. 'I'm only sorry we shan't be around to witness the transformation.'

She dropped a kiss onto Joanna's hair. 'In the meantime, if life here gets more than you can bear, you can always escape to us. I love you very much—

you and Gabriel—as if you were my own. It's hurt me to watch you tearing each other apart.' Her voice broke. 'I just wish it could have worked out differently.'

She gave a quick, sharp sigh, and was gone.

Joanna lay on her bed, staring up at the ceiling.

Sylvia's parting words still echoed and re-echoed in her mind. *'...a little girl...instead of a woman.'* Was that really how people saw her? If so, she should have made her bid for independence a long time ago.

But how could I leave? she asked herself wearily. When I was waiting for Gabriel? Hoping that he would return one day—and love me.

Because, no matter how much he had hurt her, that had always been the secret truth locked in her heart.

The demand for a divorce had been camouflage—a bit to protect herself against further wounds, to armour herself against another rejection.

But she knew now there was no safeguard strong enough to shield her from that kind of heartbreak. Within twenty-four hours of his return she'd had no defences left.

Maybe it was true. Perhaps he'd always seen her as the child he'd first known. And that was why he'd turned to Cynthia, who was all woman—beautiful, worldly and experienced.

And a Grade A, first-class bitch as well, Joanna reminded herself. But didn't they say that sex was the great deceiver? And great sex was probably the ultimate deceiver.

She wrenched her mind back from that line of thought.

At least she could make it obey her to that extent, although it still barred the way from the time of her accident to when she'd found herself here in this room.

Which was a pity, because it meant she couldn't remember being carried in Gabriel's arms. Held against his heart for the last time.

Or was her brain simply being merciful?

Faces, she thought wearily, bending over her. But the first one—the only one she'd wanted—the one she'd looked for—had been his.

Her head was aching, so she took another couple of painkillers and settled back.

What a shame her amnesia wasn't retrospective, wiping out the last three years. Giving her the chance to start again. To do everything so differently.

Only that wasn't how it worked. You got one bite of the cherry, and if you messed up there was no reprieve. No second chance.

Better not to think about that either, she told herself firmly. If she closed her eyes and tried to sleep, she might wake up with a clear head. She might remember the hill, and Gabriel's face when he found her. She might even be able to figure out what had been niggling her all day.

She was awoken an hour later by Mrs Ashby's hand, gentle on her shoulder.

'It's lunchtime, madam. I've brought you some chicken broth.'

'Oh, how lovely.' Joanna hadn't wanted much to eat over the past twenty-four hours, but now the fragrant aroma of the soup, thick with vegetables, barley and chunks of chicken, set her mouth watering.

'And here's the newspaper.' Mrs Ashby laid it beside her. 'I thought you might take a look at the crossword while you're resting.'

'You think of everything.' Joanna gave her a grateful smile as she began her soup.

She ate every mouthful, and most of the slice of mushroom quiche, still warm from the oven, which accompanied it.

Grace had even remembered to bring a pen for the crossword, she saw with amusement as she put the tray aside and reached for the paper. As she unfolded it the centre sheet came adrift and fluttered to the carpet.

'Damn.' Joanna leaned over the side of the bed to retrieve it, and stopped dead as the puzzle which had been tormenting her suddenly clicked into place.

Cynthia, she thought, recalling their conversation of the previous day. Cynthia knew that Nutkin had been spooked by a newspaper. But how? I never told her. I never told anyone. The only person who knew about it had been there at the time.

And, as if a key had been turned into her brain, another door opened into her memory.

She remembered lying bruised and winded on the short grass, her head swimming, dimly aware of someone standing over her.

Gabriel, she'd thought thankfully, turning her head slightly. Trying to find words to tell him she was all right. Forcing her reluctant eyelids open so that she could see him.

Only it hadn't been Gabriel at all.

Joanna sat bolt-upright on the bed as she recalled exactly whose face had been looking down at her.

My God, she thought numbly, her stomach churning. It was Paul Gordon.

CHAPTER TWELVE

SHE wasn't supposed to be driving. The doctor had specified a couple of days' inactivity to give her battered frame time to heal.

But there were questions to which she needed answers, and she wasn't prepared to wait.

She drove straight to the Lodge. There was no smoke coming from the chimney today, Joanna noted as she parked the car and got out.

She rapped on the front door, but there was no reply. After a brief hesitation, she tried the handle, and, to her surprise, the door swung open.

She walked into the living room and looked round, stripping off her gloves. There were dead ashes in the grate, and a number of half-filled cartons in the room, indicating that Paul Gordon's departure was already under way.

She stood for a moment, listening intently, but there was no sound except a tap dripping in the small kitchen.

Wherever he'd gone, he'd left in a hurry.

She knew exactly what she was looking for, but there was no sign of it downstairs, so she went up to the bedroom to hunt, wrinkling her nose at the wrinkled, frowsty sheets on the unmade bed.

Wherever he is, he has it with him, she concluded.

As she descended the stairs the front door opened and a man came in, his figure a dark outline against the pale wintry sunlight flooding into the hall. Joanna checked instantly, a hand flying to her throat.

Caught in the act, she thought sickly. And no way out. She'd have to try and bluff.

He kicked the door shut behind him, blocking out the concealing sunlight, and she saw who it really was.

A gasp, half-relief, half-incredulity, escaped her.

'Gabriel.'

'Yes.' He stood hands on hips, looking up at her, the dark face inimical. 'I was just leaving Sylvia's house when I saw you drive up. I couldn't believe it. You're bruised from head to foot, but you still can't keep away from him.' He looked past her. 'Where have you left him—in bed?'

'Are you mad?'

'I think that's my line.' Suddenly he looked very weary, his mouth set in bitter lines. 'Jo, he's no bloody good. I suppose I'd be bound to say that—but in his case it's true. My poor love, he's a con man. He's setting you up.'

'Wrong.' She shook her head. 'He's knocking me down. Gabriel, when I met him on the hill yesterday he was wearing a cream silk scarf. And when I was on the ground he was right there, beside me. But he didn't try to help. He just—left me there.'

'But why should he do that?' The amber eyes narrowed.

She said quietly, 'You thought there was something between us. There never was. I—I just let you think so.'

'And did he think so too?' The question was rapped at her.

Joanna nodded miserably. 'But I let him know at once that I wasn't interested. Only he—took some convincing, and he wasn't pleased.'

Gabriel said grimly, 'I could almost feel sorry for the bastard. Go on.'

She moistened dry lips with the tip of her tongue. 'When he saw me coming on Nutkin, he must have hidden among the rocks and flown the scarf at us. He knew what scared Nutkin. He was the only one who did.' Or almost, she amended silently.

Gabriel said softly, 'And he's now forfeited my sympathy for all eternity. I think I might kill him.'

'No,' she said, urgently. 'Gabriel—please. You mustn't touch him. You were right. He isn't worth it. And he's going.'

'If you know all this—what he's capable of—why did you come here? Why did you take the risk?'

'I wanted to find the scarf. To prove that it could have happened the way I said.'

'I already knew that. You were so insistent that I went up to the Hermitage and looked among the rocks. It was muddy, and he'd left some man-size footprints.' He looked round. 'So, if he's not here, where's he gone?'

She hesitated fatally. 'I—don't know.'

'Joanna,' he said gently, 'don't lie to me. Not now. Not ever. And certainly not to protect that piece of scum.'

It's you I'm trying to protect, she wanted to shout at him. Because if my suspicions are right, you're going to be so desperately hurt. And I can't bear it...

Aloud, she said, 'I mean—I can't be sure.'

He said, 'Then let's go and make sure,' and opened the front door. 'We'll take my car.'

'But you don't know where we're going,' she protested as she preceded him out of the Lodge.

He said, 'Ah, but I do.' And his voice was colder than ice.

*   *   *

Larkspur Cottage looked deserted too, but Cynthia's car was parked in the lean-to garage.

Gabriel's face looked as if it had been chiselled from marble. Joanna ached for him as they went up the path.

She said in a whisper, 'Suppose the door is locked this time.'

'I have a key.'

'Yes,' she said bravely. 'I—I'd forgotten.' She drew a deep breath. 'Gabriel, we don't have to do this.'

He said almost gently, 'Yes, Joanna, we do have to.' He fitted the key into the lock and turned it. The door opened noiselessly and they stepped into the flagged hall. There was an oak chest against one wall, and across it was lying a black leather coat—and a cream silk scarf.

Joanna bit her lip until she could taste blood. She supposed that for Gabriel's sake she'd been praying it wasn't true. That she'd added two and two and come up with millions. She hardly dared look at him.

She could hear the distant murmur of voices coming from upstairs, and Cynthia's unmistakable giggle.

He said, 'Go and wait in the car, Jo.'

'What are you going to do?' Her voice was breathless. 'Nothing silly—or dangerous—promise me?'

'I'll do what's necessary.' He turned her quietly and firmly towards the door.

She stood outside for a moment, gulping cold air into her lungs, then went down the path. As she was getting into the car she thought she heard a muffled shriek, then a distant crash, and realised she was shaking.

It seemed like an eternity before Gabriel came out of the cottage and joined her in the car. He was walking normally, and she couldn't see any bloodstains, although the knuckles on one hand looked sore.

She said, 'Well?'

'Gordon's going back to London tomorrow. Your stepmother will be leaving too.' He started the car.

She said, 'I see.' She hesitated. 'Has—has it been going on long?'

'She's known him for years. It seems he was some kind of toy boy.' His voice was flat. 'The relationship has been on an on-off basis ever since.'

'Even while she was married to my father?' Joanna felt sick.

'I would guess as much.'

She bit her lip. 'They—they must care about each other—if he came down here especially to be with her.'

Gabriel's mouth hardened. 'That wasn't entirely the reason.'

The dark face was so forbidding she didn't dare ask anything more.

What a fool Cynthia was, she thought, to risk her future for a liaison with someone as worthless as Paul Gordon.

She couldn't even guess at how Gabriel must be feeling, but the sense of betrayal had to be acute.

He must wish that neither of us had ever come near the Manor, she thought wretchedly. But at least she could relieve him of her own presence.

She cleared her throat. 'Sylvia and Charles have asked me to stay with them for a little while. I—I'd like to do that.'

There was a silence, then he said, 'That might be best. Do you want to come back to the Manor and get your things?'

'I'll do that later.' There was a hard, icy lump in

her chest. As she'd suspected, he couldn't wait to be rid of her.

Joanna lifted her chin and tried to speak normally. 'if you could drop me at the Lodge, I'll pick up my car and check with Sylvia that it's convenient for me to arrive today.'

'I'm sure it will be.' His mouth twisted. 'She always seems to have a room made up for waifs and strays.'

It wasn't a description she relished, she thought, biting her lip. But it probably summed up the situation with fair accuracy.

Sylvia's welcome was warm, and mercifully devoid of awkward questions.

It was late afternoon before Joanna felt able to give her a brief and stilted account of what had happened. Sylvia listened with pursed lips.

'Well, it explains his lifestyle, I suppose,' she commented. 'But very little else. What possessed her to allow him down here? Didn't she realise how Gabriel would react?'

Joanna bent her head unhappily. 'Perhaps she thought she wouldn't be found out.'

'Well, Charles has been down to the Lodge, and the place has been cleared out. The enterprising Mr Gordon has slung his hook,' she added inelegantly. 'Off to look for another woman with more money than sense, no doubt.'

'You don't think he'll stay with Cynthia?'

'Not since the blow to her financial prospects.' Sylvia shook her head. 'Of course, I never approved of what Gabriel was planning. I think this whole debacle has saved him a lot of problems in the future.'

But I doubt if he sees it that way, Joanna thought drearily.

'May I ring the Manor?' she asked after a moment. 'I'd like Grace to pack me a bag.'

'Of course, dear. And I'll see about some tea.'

Joanna dialled the familiar number, and waited. It rang several times before the receiver was lifted at the other end and a voice she hadn't expected to hear again, said, 'Westroe Manor. Cynthia Elcott speaking.'

'Cynthia?' Incredulity and dismay jostled in Joanna's mind. 'What are you doing there?'

Cynthia laughed unpleasantly. 'Come off it, sweetie. Did you think you were going to get rid of me that easily? Surely not. I'm here to kiss and make up with Gabriel.'

'You really believe he'll forgive you?'

'Why not? He's a man of the world—and the pot can hardly call the kettle black. After all, I turned a blind eye to his little diversion with you the other night. I knew he'd be expecting me, and I was right. He's even arranged it so that we have the house to ourselves, without you behaving like the skeleton at the feast. Wasn't that tactful of him?'

She paused. 'What do you want, anyway?'

'I wanted to arrange to fetch some clothes.'

'All taken care of, darling. Gabriel told Mrs Ashby to pack everything up, and her husband's bringing it all across to you.'

'Everything?' Joanna asked, dry-mouthed.

'All your treasured possessions. I don't think he wants you to have any excuse to call round.' She laughed again. 'So make sure you take the hint and stay away from now on. Pretty please?'

And Joanna heard the phone go down.

* * *

'It's no good,' Joanna said firmly. 'I have to start looking for somewhere to live.'

Sylvia sighed. 'I don't think you should rush into anything. You've only been here a week, and you're still looking peaky,' she said sternly, surveying Joanna as if she was a plant that had failed to bloom. 'Don't forget that nasty attack of delayed shock you had on the day you arrived.'

Joanna gave a constricted smile. 'I haven't forgotten.' It had been the only excuse she could think of when Sylvia had returned with the tea and found her stretched out on the sofa, weeping broken-heartedly and unable to stop, she recalled ruefully.

She still cried, but only into her pillow at night. During the daytime she managed to put a brave face on things.

Her luggage had duly arrived, and, as Cynthia had said, nothing had been forgotten. She'd seen Sylvia and Charles exchanging astonished looks as Mr Ashby carried the cases into the hall.

For the first few days she'd jumped each time the phone rang, wondering if it might be Gabriel calling to offer some explanation, or at least to say goodbye.

But as time went by without a word from him she realised there was nothing to hope for. And how could she complain? She was the one who'd demanded the clean break originally.

But I didn't mean it, she thought desolately. He'd hurt me, and I wanted to hurt him back. To make him think I was over him. That I didn't care any more. When, in reality, not a day passed that I didn't think about him and want him back at any price.

And now I've lost him for ever.

Sometimes she wondered if Charles and Sylvia had heard about Cynthia's triumphant return. Certainly there was no hint from either of them that they knew she was installed as mistress at the manor.

No doubt they would come to terms with the situation in their own way. And it would ease things if Joanna was no longer around to divide their loyalties from Gabriel.

The problem was that she had no idea where she wanted to go.

Somewhere with hills, and sky, she thought, where early primroses grow in sheltered hollows. Somewhere I can walk, and ride, and heal myself. And learn, somehow, to forget.

The next morning, at breakfast, there was a letter for her from Henry Fortescue.

There were papers for her to sign, regarding the financial settlement she had agreed with Gabriel. Perhaps she would telephone him to make the necessary appointment.

He was his usual friendly, businesslike self when she rang.

'Not tomorrow morning, I'm afraid,' he said, when she diffidently suggested a time. 'I shall be at the Manor for the discussions with the Furnival Hotels representatives.' He paused. 'No doubt you're aware of their interest?'

'Yes.' She kept her voice steady.

'But I shall be free after lunch. Shall we say three p.m. at my office?'

She agreed quietly, and rang off. So the final chapter in Westroe Manor's history was about to be written, she thought unhappily. And Cynthia's victory was complete and entire.

The next day she told Charles and Sylvia she was going out, ostensibly to make contact with a firm of estate agents in Westroe with branches all over the country.

In reality, she drove up onto the hill, parked the car at the small plantation, which was a gathering point for ramblers, and walked the mile along the ridge to the Hermitage.

One last look, she vowed. And perfectly safe, because everyone at the house would be busy at the meeting.

It was milder today, and sunny, with a gentle breeze that murmured among the stones. She unbuttoned her coat as she leaned back against one of the rocks.

'Joanna.'

For a moment she thought she was fantasising. Hearing Gabriel's voice in the song of the breeze. She looked slowly round and saw him, standing a few yards away, his hands thrust into his coat pockets, his dark hair ruffled by the wind.

She said wildly, 'You—what are you doing here?'

'I came to find you.'

'But you didn't know I was here,' she protested. 'You couldn't have done. I didn't tell a soul.'

He said quietly, 'But I knew just the same. As I've always known.'

She was burning up with embarrassment. 'I'm sorry,' she mumbled. 'I didn't mean to intrude. I thought you'd be tied up in your meeting.'

Gabriel shook his head. 'I cancelled it.'

'Cancelled?' she echoed dazedly. 'But why?'

'Because I realised I wasn't prepared to let it go,' he said. 'Not while there was the remotest chance I could still make the life I'd dreamed of become a reality.'

She'd hoped for this change of heart, so why couldn't she rejoice in it?

She said steadily, 'And can it come true?'

'That,' he said, 'depends on the woman I love.'

She swallowed. 'I suppose you've—talked to her about it?'

'No. Communications between us seem to have broken down.'

In other words, Cynthia didn't want to know, she thought sadly.

She tried a pitiful attempt at a smile. 'Then perhaps you ought to find another dream.'

'Not easy. I've carried this one with me for too long. Cherished it through some bitter times. Clung to it when there seemed no hope at all.' He shook his head. 'I'm not going to give it up, no matter how long it stays just a dream.'

'Then talk to her.' She forced the words out somehow. 'Tell her how you feel.'

'I'm scared, Joanna. Scared of screwing up again. I thought I could let her go. I wanted to—but I can't. She's in my blood—in my bones. Without her, there's no life at all.'

She said hoarsely, raggedly, 'Don't tell me these things—please. I can't bear any more...' There were tears in her throat, scalding her, choking her. 'Oh, God, I should never have come here.'

His voice was suddenly fierce. 'You came here for the same reason that I did. Because you couldn't keep away. Because you needed to find me.'

'No.' There were tears on her face now, burning their way into her skin. 'No, you mustn't say that. I won't listen.'

'I'll make you listen. Wherever you go, I'll come after you. Whatever you do, I'll be there. Because without you I'm incomplete.'

He threw back his head. His face looked hunted,

vulnerable. 'I've tried so hard to do the right thing, Jo—to give you the freedom you've never had. That's why I overruled Lionel's will.'

He sighed. 'He wanted us to get back together so badly. He thought if you had to stay in the house, maybe some miracle would happen. But then I saw the effect it was having on you, and I knew I had to release you.

'I wanted you to be independent—to live your life on your own terms. At the same time I hoped, if I was patient, that some day in the future you'd find room for me there.

'But I can't let you go, Joanna. I'm too selfish—and too frightened. I'm terrified you'll meet some nice guy who'll never give you a moment's grief, and that you'll settle down with him and be content. But he'll never take you to the heights, Jo. He'll never think his way into your mind, or uplift your soul. And when you're lost, he won't know where to look. And he'll never love you as I do.'

She pressed herself against the rock, her whole body shaking.

'Cynthia,' she whispered. 'You love Cynthia. You talked about her. About marrying again.'

'Cynthia,' he said, slowly and clearly, 'is a poisonous bitch. She always was and always will be. Lionel saw it from the start. That's why he put on the pressure for us to marry, because he was worried about the kind of influence she might exert on you. But, whatever she was planning in that tortuous brain of hers, my sole aim has been to get her out of our lives, no matter what the cost. That's why I let her take whatever furnishings she fancied. I thought she'd get fed up with living at the cottage and move on, without the necessity of a big showdown.'

'But she came back to the Manor that afternoon. I spoke to her on the telephone.'

'Oh, yes, she came back.' His voice was rough. 'She seemed to be expecting some kind of pay-off, as an inducement for her to leave us in peace. I showed her the error of her ways, and subsequently the door. I suspect we've seen the last of her, and her revolting boyfriend.'

'She told me you'd had all my clothes packed and were sending Mr Ashby round with them.'

'Indeed?' he said carefully. 'Now she told Mrs Ashby that you'd asked for everything to be sent to Charles and Sylvia's. I wasn't even consulted.'

She gave a shaky laugh. 'Manipulative to the end.'

'You don't know the half of it.' His mouth tightened. 'She hired Paul Gordon to come down here, Jo. He was intended to seduce you—drive a wedge between us and clear the way for her.'

Her lips parted in a silent gasp. 'You're not serious.'

'Never more so. They genuinely tried to set you up. They admitted it. Gordon felt he'd have succeeded too, but for your inherent frigidity. Although he expressed it rather differently,' he added harshly. 'He also admitted making you fall off Nutkin. To bring you down a peg or two, I gather.'

She remembered his bruised knuckles. 'I hope you hit him hard.'

His smile was wintry, his eyes bleak. 'You know I did, lady.'

She looked down at the ground. 'But you stayed away so much, especially at night. I thought you were with her. At the cottage.'

He shook his head. 'I used to go to Charles and Sylvia.' His mouth twisted in a faint smile. 'I was the original waif and stray. The truth was, I didn't trust myself to be alone with you.'

Colour rose in her face. She said hurriedly, 'And you kept talking about your new wife—about not making the same mistakes again. I was sure you meant her.'

Gabriel said very gently, 'I was talking about you, Jo. God, I was even prepared to let you divorce me, so that we could start completely afresh. So that I could court you properly, as I should have done the first time. If you remember, when I married you, I'd hardly kissed you, let alone laid a hand on you.'

'I didn't think you wanted me...'

'How wrong can you be?' His voice was husky. 'I was crazy for you—but you were so young—so innocent. And the fact that we'd been living under the same roof didn't help. I wasn't sure you weren't confusing the term ''husband'' with some kind of elder brother. And the last thing I'd felt for some time was brotherly,' he added, with a touch of grimness.

'But I meant to woo you very gently—to give you as much time as you needed. And then, on our wedding night, I just lost it completely. Treated you as if I'd bought you. I knew I was hurting you—scaring you—and I couldn't bloody stop...' He shook his head. 'I thought the look in your eyes was going to haunt me for the rest of my life.

'Every time we were in bed together, I felt as if you were—enduring me. I couldn't forgive myself for what I'd done to you, and then I almost got to a point where I couldn't forgive you either—so I decided to get out. To give us both some breathing space, then try again.'

She said, 'I thought you were just bored. That my lack of experience irritated you.'

'I had never in my life known such sweetness.' His voice was almost reverent. 'And not being able to reach you was the worst kind of torture. Like having the gates of paradise slammed in your face.'

She said shyly, 'I did want you. But I think, perhaps, I was afraid—not just of you—but of being a woman. Your woman.'

He was very still. 'Are you still afraid?'

'No,' she said. 'Are you?'

'A little, maybe.' He drew a ragged breath. 'Scared that I'll reach for you, only to have you draw back again.'

'In that case,' she said. 'I'll come to you.'

It was only a short distance, but it could have divided them for ever.

She stood in front of him, her eyes lifted gravely to his, recognising the tenderness—the need in their tawny glow.

She said, 'I love you, Gabriel. I always have. I always will. Please let me share your dream.'

His arms closed round her, pulling her against him, and their lips met, heatedly, fiercely. They kissed until they were breathless, half-laughing, half-crying. Then they drew slightly apart and stood for a moment, looking at each other, acknowledging a mutual longing too strong to be denied for another minute.

Gabriel took her hand and led her into the shelter of the stones to a place where new grass was springing. Silently he took off his coat and spread it on the ground, drawing her down with him to lie in his arms. He kissed her again, slowly, almost druggingly, his tongue playing with hers.

At the same time Joanna was aware that his hands had penetrated her layers of clothing and were exploring, very delicately, her naked breasts. And that her body was melting deliciously in response. She controlled a little gasp.

'Are you cold?' Gabriel touched his lips to the pulse beneath her ear.

'No,' she managed. His hand was under her skirt now, stroking her sweetly, languorously, making it difficult for her to breathe. Or indeed to do anything except arch her body in mute demand against his sensuous fingers.

He whispered unevenly, 'Joanna, my sweet, my only love, do you really want me at last?'

'Yes.' Her hands moved on him feverishly, freeing him from the confines of his clothing. 'Oh, Gabriel— yes.'

The last fragile barriers between them were soon stripped away. She lifted herself eagerly to meet him—to welcome him into her—all inhibitions gone.

As she felt the heat, the strength of him fill her, Joanna gave a tiny moan of pleasure.

His hands cupped her face. His voice was hoarse. 'Did I hurt you, darling. Did I?'

'No.' She smiled up at him, gloriously, triumphantly, feeling her body tighten round him. 'Just— love me...'

He began to move inside her, slowly at first, controlling himself for her pleasure. Hands clinging to his shoulders, her legs wrapped round his hips, Joanna abandoned herself to the rhythm of their passion, flesh of his flesh and bone of his bone.

She could feel heat building inside her, a dizzying spiral of sensation which lifted and carried her like some tidal wave to a moment where all thought ceased and her body shuddered in pure physical rapture to its climax.

She cried out in aching delight, and heard Gabriel answer her as he reached his own culmination.

Aeons later... 'I should have done this three years ago,' Gabriel murmured into her hair. 'Brought you up here with a bottle of champagne, staged the world's most complete seduction, and then, but only then, asked you to marry me.'

'Why didn't you?' Joanna stroked his cheek with her hand.

He sighed. 'Lionel had pretty well forbidden it, for one thing. He had old-fashioned views about virgin brides. But mostly because I was scared that you wouldn't want to come with me—that you'd say no.' He lifted his head and looked at her gravely. 'Would you have done?'

'I don't know,' she told him honestly. 'Perhaps I wasn't brave enough—or mature enough—to give you what you wanted then. Maybe this is the route we had to take to find each other.'

He kissed her gently on the mouth and sat up. 'And now we'd better take the quickest route home, before we get pneumonia. I think we should spend the rest of the day in bed, don't you?'

'We can't,' Joanna said, stricken. 'I'm supposed to see Henry at three o'clock.'

'No, you're not,' he said, grimacing. 'You were going to see me, actually. That was my fall-back plan, just in case you didn't show this morning.'

'And you call other people manipulative.' Joanna let him help her to her feet. 'Anyway, what would Mrs Ashby think?'

'That we'd come to our senses at last.' Gabriel traced the outline of her parted lips with a fingertip. 'Then she'll put some champagne on ice. And after that she'll go up to the attic and get my old cot down. She's mentioned it several times lately.'

'Is that part of your dream?' Joanna's eyes were luminous, her smile very tender.

He kissed her again. 'You, our home, love, laughter and babies. That sums it up.'

'Sounds good to me.' She stood on tiptoe and kissed him. 'My angel.'

Gabriel took her in his arms and held her for a long moment, safe and secure against his heart.

Then, hand in hand, together at last, they walked down the hill to their heritage.

MILLS & BOON

Next Month's Romances

♡

Each month you can choose from a wide variety of romance novels from Mills & Boon®. Below are the new titles to look out for next month from the Presents™ and Enchanted™ series.

Presents™

OUTBACK HEAT	Emma Darcy
HONEYMOON BABY	Susan Napier
GIORDANNI'S PROPOSAL	Jacqueline Baird
THE BABY BOND	Sharon Kendrick
MAN ABOUT THE HOUSE	Alison Kelly
THE IDEAL FATHER	Rosalie Ash
BRIDE FOR SALE	Susanne McCarthy
ANYONE BUT YOU	Jennifer Crusie

Enchanted™

THE TEMPTATION TRAP	Catherine George
THE DIAMOND DAD	Lucy Gordon
ONE BRIDE REQUIRED!	Emma Richmond
LOOK-ALIKE FIANCÉE	Elizabeth Duke
HEAVENLY HUSBAND	Carolyn Greene
HIS PERFECT PARTNER	Laura Martin
MAIL-ORDER MOTHER	Kate Denton
AND BABY MAKES SIX	Pamela Dalton

On sale from 11th September 1998

H1 9808

Available at most branches of
WH Smith, John Menzies, Martins, Tesco, Asda, Volume One, Sainsbury and Safeway

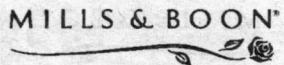

W ORD 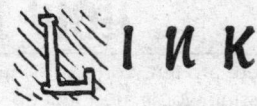L I N K

We are giving away a year's supply of Mills & Boon® books to the five lucky winners of our latest competition. Simply fill in the ten missing words below, complete the coupon overleaf and send this entire page to us by 28th February 1999. The first five correct entries will each win a year's subscription to the Mills & Boon series of their choice. What could be easier?

BUSINESS	**SUIT**	CASE
BOTTLE		HAT
FRONT		BELL
PARTY		BOX
SHOE		PIPE
RAIN		TIE
ARM		MAN
SIDE		ROOM
BEACH		GOWN
FOOT		KIND
BIRTHDAY		BOARD

Please turn over for details of how to enter ⇨

C8H

HOW TO ENTER

There are ten words missing from our list overleaf. Each of the missing words must link up with the two on either side to make a new word or words.

For example, 'Business' links with 'Suit' and 'Case' to form 'Business Suit' and 'Suit Case':

BUSINESS—SUIT—CASE

As you find each one, write it in the space provided. When you have linked up all the words, fill in the coupon below, pop this page into an envelope and post it today. Don't forget you could win a year's supply of Mills & Boon® books—you don't even need to pay for a stamp!

Mills & Boon Word Link Competition
FREEPOST CN81, Croydon, Surrey, CR9 3WZ

EIRE readers: (please affix stamp) PO Box 4546, Dublin 24.

Please tick the series you would like to receive if you are one of the lucky winners

Presents™ ❏   Enchanted™ ❏   Medical Romance™ ❏
Historical Romance™ ❏   Temptation®

Are you a Reader Service™ subscriber?   Yes ❏   No ❏

Ms/Mrs/Miss/Mr ....Initials...........................
(BLOCK CAPITALS PLEASE)

Surname...

Address ....

....

.............................Postcode...........................

(I am over 18 years of age)   C8H

Closing date for entries is 28th February 1999.
One entry per household. Competition open to residents of the UK and Ireland only. You may be mailed with offers from other reputable companies as a result of this application. If you would prefer not to receive such offers, please tick this box. ❏

Mills & Boon is a registered trademark
owned by Harlequin Mills & Boon Limited